MARK OF THE CYCLOPS

AN ANCIENT GREEK MYSTERY

Bloomsbury Education
An imprint of Bloomsbury Publishing Plc

50 Bedford Square   1385 Broadway
London   New York
WC1B 3DP   NY 10018
UK   USA

www.bloomsbury.com

BLOOMSBURY and the Diana logo are trademarks of Bloomsbury Publishing Plc

First published in 2017

A catalogue record for this book is available from the British Library.

ISBN
PB: 978-1-4729-3414-7
ePub: 978-1-4729-3416-1
ePDF: 978-1-4729-3417-8

2 4 6 8 10 9 7 5 3 1

Typeset by Newgen Knowledge Works (P) Ltd., Chennai, India
Printed and bound by CPI Group (UK) Ltd, Croydon CR0 4YY

This book is produced using paper that is made from wood grown in managed, sustainable forests.
It is natural, renewable and recyclable. The logging and manufacturing processes conform to the
environmental regulations of the country of origin.

To find out more about our authors and books visit www.bloomsbury.com.
Here you will find extracts, author interviews, details of forthcoming
events and the option to sign up for our newsletters.

MARK OF THE CYCLOPS

AN ANCIENT GREEK MYSTERY

SAVIOUR PIROTTA

Illustrated by FREYA HARTAS

BLOOMSBURY EDUCATION
AN IMPRINT OF BLOOMSBURY

LONDON OXFORD NEW YORK NEW DELHI SYDNEY

For my brother Lino
With fond memories of all the long, lazy summers
spent reading The Famous Five or Biggles and longing
for almond granita.

CONTENTS

ISTHMUS
OF CORINTH

ATHENS

CORINTH

AEGEAN SEA

CRETE

CHAPTER ONE

A New Slave for Master Ariston

I knew Thrax would be brilliant at solving mysteries the very first time we spoke. It was the morning after the spring festival and I had gone running to work off some of the rich food I'd eaten. When I returned home, there was a boy with a newly shaved head – the mark of a slave – coming out of the kitchen. I guessed Master Lykos had just bought him at the festival. He seemed to be a year or two older than me and was carrying a water jar.

'Give us some water,' I gasped. 'My throat's drier than a rubble wall.'

The boy handed me the jar. He had the darkest, most intense eyes I'd ever seen.

'You must be a scribe,' he said.

'How do you know that?' I asked, knowing I had no ink stains on my hands.

'You have scrubbed your fingers too hard,' he chuckled while I gulped water straight from the jar. 'They are still raw. And I can detect a faint whiff of pine sap coming off you. That's one of the ingredients in ink – you mix glue made from the sap of pine trees with soot and water. It's in your hair.'

'I did fill up a fresh pot of ink before my run this morning,' I admitted as I handed back the water jar. 'And I have a habit of running my fingers through my hair when it gets too long. By the golden chariot of Apollo, I've never met anyone so observant. I wouldn't want you on my tail if I'd broken the law.' I stuck out my right hand. 'My name's Nicomachus, but everyone calls me Nico.'

The boy returned the greeting, pumping my hand so hard I nearly winced. 'Master Lykos has decided to call me Thrax,' he said. 'It's a good name, I think. A lot of wrestlers are called Thrax.'

'Welcome to the house,' I said.

'Master Lykos said I'm going to be a personal slave to his son.'

'That would be Master Ariston,' I said. 'He's a professional singer and travels around, performing at weddings and festivals. He writes his own poems and songs too, and plays the lyre. If you're going to be his personal slave, we'll be seeing a lot of each other. I'm his scribe.'

'Does Master Ariston treat you well?' asked Thrax.

'I'm a freeborn apprentice,' I replied, 'but my life's not much better than a slave's. Not that I'm complaining. Life in this house is very comfortable. Master Lykos likes to bark at everyone but deep down he's very kind. The entire household gets to sleep in warm beds and there's always enough food.'

I didn't tell Thrax that Master Lykos also sold off one or two slaves every autumn festival; the ones who didn't obey his every word or cost too much in food and clothing.

By now the sun had fully risen and the courtyard was getting hot. 'I must go and clean myself up before Master Ariston comes back from his morning visit to the barber,' I said.

'And I must hurry indoors with this water,' said Thrax. 'Mistress has set me scrubbing Master Ariston's sandals and boots but she keeps interrupting me to fetch things. I've never seen anyone with so much footwear as Master Ariston. He's got a chest full of it. It's my first job in the house and I think it's going to take all day.'

I started towards the bathroom, which was on the ground floor. Master Lykos's house is very traditional. All the rooms overlook a central courtyard with an altar to the gods and grape vines growing up the walls.

'I'll see you this evening at supper, Thrax,' I called as he hurried up the stairs with the water.

Master Lykos stuck his head out of his bedroom window. He was a thick-set man with jowly cheeks that wobbled when he spoke. 'What's all this shouting for?' he bellowed. 'Can't a man have breakfast in peace?'

*   *   *

When Master Ariston returned from the barber's, he asked me to write down a rambling poem about roses, the symbol of love. We were off to a very important wedding in Corinth soon and he was busy composing romantic songs for it. My job was to write down the verses as they spilled out of his mouth. Once in a while, he'd ask me to read them back to him and he'd make changes and corrections.

The household cook brought fresh barley bread and figs for lunch, which Master Ariston and I ate at the writing table. We worked through supper too so there was no opportunity for me to see Thrax again till bedtime.

I might be a freeman but, as a lowly scribe, I still sleep in the same room as the other male slaves. In our house that's the storeroom near the front door. I suppose we sleep there in case robbers attack the house at night and we are needed to defend the women. Not that I would be much use against violent robbers. Despite my early morning runs and occasional trips to the gym, I find it difficult to keep my weight down.

Thrax, on the other hand, looked like he could give a professional athlete a run for his money. As he patted down the straw on his low wooden bed, I could see he was lean with not an ounce of fat on him.

'Did you have a good day?' I asked.

Thrax plumped up his straw pillow. 'It turned out to be surprisingly easy. Cleaning Master Ariston's boots and sandals didn't take as long as I feared. Then I was sent to the market with another slave to have a pair of sandals mended, and to get Master Ariston one of those heavy woollen cloaks that swirl around your ankles. Himations, I think they're called. Master

Ariston has as many himations as he has pairs of boots. I must say, the life of a slave is much easier in the city than the country.'

'Is that where you used to live?' I asked, getting into my own bed.

'I belonged to a farmer outside Thebes for ten years,' replied Thrax. 'He was a kind man but last autumn the crops failed and he had to sell some of us to pay his debts.'

'Were you born a slave?'

Thrax ran his hand over his smooth head. 'No. My father was a freeman from Thrace. A silversmith by trade, quite a successful one I think. We lived in a small house built right in the city walls. There was a picture of a glaring Medusa painted above our front door to ward off evil. I don't remember much about my father, just that he was very tall. He died when I was young. I do remember my mum's face clearly, though. I can still feel her soft lips against my cheeks when she kissed me.'

Just then the other two male slaves in our household came in to make up their beds and

Thrax stopped talking. Being reminded of his early years must have changed his mood for he didn't say another word before he wished me goodnight and blew out his lamp.

As I lay on my straw, listening to everyone snoring, I wondered how Thrax had become a slave. Had he been kidnapped by pirates? Had his mother been forced to sell him into slavery to pay off her husband's debts? I shuddered to think how painful losing your family and freedom must be and I offered a quick prayer to the gods for my own good luck.

Although my parents are poor farmers from the island of Kos, I was lucky enough to be schooled for free by a temple scribe. He'd noticed me scribbling letters in the soil with a broken reed one day and offered me an apprenticeship. Now I make enough money to send a little to my parents twice a year. Because of me they have a roof over their heads and warm food in their bellies.

But things might have turned out very differently had I not met that kind scribe. I might have become a penniless farmer trying to eke out a meagre living from the dusty land. Or my parents might have had to sell me into slavery too.

Shortly before dawn I was woken by the sound of muttering. I opened my eyes to see Thrax sitting up in his bed. His shaved head was glistening with sweat and his fists were balled up tight against his chin.

'Are you all right?' I whispered.

Thrax turned but I could see from the glazed expression in his eyes that he wasn't looking at me. He was having a nightmare.

'I'll return, Mother,' he hissed. 'I'll come back and find you. As soon as I buy my freedom. I promise!'

CHAPTER TWO

Of Mice and Sailors

We started out for the wedding in Corinth a few days later. There were three of us going: Master Ariston, Thrax and me.

Master Lykos wasn't keen on his only son going to a city he considered full of greedy businessmen and drunken sailors.

'Everyone there is a traitor to the Greek spirit,' he grumbled as he offered sacrifice to Hermes at the household altar. 'They've been at war with the island of Corcyra for two years, though I hear Athens might come to the island's rescue any day now. And what if war was declared while you were there? You might be denounced as a spy and pushed to your death off a cliff.'

'The fighting is happening at sea a long way from Corinth, Father, and well you know it,' laughed Master Ariston. He was a thin, gawky fellow with big ears and a puny chest, but he had a surprisingly loud voice. 'Our host is Zenon the Younger, one of the most respected merchants in the city. His eldest daughter Pandora is marrying the son of a much-admired colonel. A champion runner called Sosicles. There will be influential people at the wedding from all over Hellas. It'll be good for business.'

'Business,' thundered Master Lykos, who was a retired trierarch. 'I remember when Athens depended on nothing more than a brief, exciting war and a spot of olive farming in the winter.'

'Goodbye, Father,' said Ariston as Thrax opened the front gate. 'Keep offering sacrifices to fast-footed Hermes that he might bring us back home safely.'

He looked up at the terrace on the second floor where a woman stood watching. 'Give us your hand in blessing, Mother, so that Athena may look upon our journey with favour. We'll bring you back something nice.'

Ariston's Mother nodded and raised her hand. Then we all trooped out of the house and down the street, Ariston sitting sideways on a donkey. He wore a wide-brimmed hat to protect his face from the sun and carried his precious lyre in a cedar-wood box on his lap.

The donkey, a sweet furry creature called Ariana, also carried a large wicker chest strapped to her side. It was packed full of the master's clothes and footwear as well as a miniature bronze statue of Apollo. Master Ariston's dedication to the god knew no bounds and he travelled everywhere with the statue, to which he prayed and offered sacrifice every night.

Thrax was weighed down with a second chest lashed to his back. It contained a huge pile of scrolls, an entire library that Master Ariston carried everywhere.

As a freeman, I was not required to carry anything for Master Ariston. Instead I had a bag slung over my shoulder filled with the tools of my trade: a kalamos to write on papyrus, styluses for working on a wax tablet and small blocks of dried ink.

We could have travelled to Corinth by land, joining pilgrims on their way to a famous temple of Poseidon on the outskirts of the city. Master Ariston however had a great fear of wild animals and much preferred travelling by sea. He had booked us passage on a small cargo ship called the *Danais*. It was sailing out of Piraeus, a harbour on the outskirts of Athens, and it would take us all the way down the Saronic Gulf to the Isthmus of Corinth in southern Hellas.

The ship's captain was an old friend of Master Ariston's called Gorgos. They'd had the same tutor as kids, and they still drank together to his memory whenever the *Danais* was in port.

We were not the only fee-paying passengers on the ship. A very fat man from Corinth was also travelling with us. He had the bushiest eyebrows

I had ever seen and spoke with an unexpectedly high-pitched voice. He introduced himself as Odius the Elder.

'Don't you dare laugh at him,' whispered Master Ariston, while we found Ariana a safe spot on the ship. 'He is one of the archons in Corinth.'

'What's an archon?' asked Thrax.

'A powerful magistrate,' I explained. 'Every city-state has them. They are in charge of the law, the army and the temples. They even organise festivals.'

A pottery merchant called Peleas and his Nubian slave, Tanoutamon, were also on the ship. Peleas knew Master Ariston too and was really pleased to see him.

'I believe one or two of my more expensive pieces are destined for the wedding you're attending,' said Peleas as Tanoutamon and two other slaves stowed the pots in the hold. 'A grand affair it's going to be from what I hear. How are things with you, old friend?'

'I thank Apollo for bringing me good fortune,' answered Master Ariston. 'I have bookings all over Hellas and I am blessed with a new personal slave.'

'The gods favour me too,' said Peleas. 'Business is booming and I have taken on a very talented new painter. His name is Scorpius. He signs his pots with a little scorpion, drawn at the base.'

The passengers continued chatting as the *Danais* was unmoored and the crew pushed her away from the quay with their oars. She had both a sail and six strong rowers, who had brought their own oars and cushions to sit on. They manoeuvered us deftly out of the harbour and, with a strong wind behind us, Captain Gorgos soon raised the sail.

The oarsmen relaxed and began sharing gossip and news of their families. Their voices got louder as they spoke and before long we realised that two of them were quarrelling.

It seemed, on a previous voyage, the men had found some mice nesting behind a sack of almonds. They had tamed them and taught them to do simple tricks. One by one the mice had died

or tumbled overboard into the sea. Now there was only one left and two men both claimed they owned it.

'I must nip this quarrel in the bud,' Captain Gorgos said to Master Ariston as they stood with the archon and Peleas at the prow of the *Danais*. 'Small arguments like these can easily turn into big fights.'

'Yes,' agreed the archon gravely. 'A ship needs harmony to run smoothly. You must get rid of the man who's lying or he'll bring the wrath of Poseidon on you.'

Captain Gorgos frowned. 'But how do I know which man is telling the truth?'

'If I may be so bold, sir,' said Thrax, who was serving Master Ariston a cup of wine. 'I can help you solve the problem.'

Captain Gorgos looked at Thrax hopefully. 'How?'

'Tell the men that unless they settle their dispute right away, you will throw the mouse overboard,' said Thrax. 'I think you'll find the liar will soon be unmasked.'

Captain Gorgos whistled loudly to get the men's attention and asked to see the mouse. One of the quarrelling rowers handed it to him, holding it gently by the tail.

'I cannot have this kind of bickering on my ship,' announced the captain. 'Unless you can decide who really owns the little fellow, he is going overboard.'

'I agree, sir,' said the first man. 'This kind of fighting angers Poseidon. Chuck the mouse into the sea.'

'No, don't,' cried the second man, the one who'd passed the mouse to the captain. 'Let my colleague here keep him. I swear on the life of my children I won't argue about the matter again.'

'I think you'll find the second man is the real owner of the mouse,' Thrax whispered to Captain Gorgos. 'He'd rather see his pet go to another than be drowned.'

Captain Gorgos handed the mouse to its rightful owner, who stowed it inside his chiton. The archon and Peleas looked at Thrax with a mixture of surprise and admiration.

'It's a crying shame you're a slave, young man,' said the archon, 'or you could have a glorious career in politics. If you ever buy your freedom come and see me. I could do with an intelligent man like you in my service.'

'Or you could come and work for me,' added Peleas. 'I bet you'd be excellent at selling expensive vases.'

Ha! As if Thrax should waste his time compiling reports for the archon, or selling pots for a commission. He was proving to have a brilliant mind and I was sure he could put it to better use than that.

Later in the day, we were settling down to a small meal of olives and bread when the archon cried, 'Captain Gorgos, look!'

We all looked up from our food to see a small one-masted ship making its way towards us. It was soon joined by two more, which seemed to appear out of nowhere.

'They're pirates,' said Peleas.

Thrax and I both looked at him in alarm. 'How do you know?'

'They're coming from the direction of Aegina,' replied Peleas. 'It's an island known as a hideout for pirates. And they're all heading towards us. They mean to take our cargo.'

'And they'll take us too,' wailed Master Ariston. 'I might end up a slave.'

'The lord god Poseidon, protector of all who sail the seas, help us,' whispered the archon.

'Aye, may he help us, your honour,' said Captain Gorgos. 'But we need to help ourselves too. Please sit down and let my crew do their work.' He turned to his men. 'Put your back to it, lads, if you want to see your families again.'

The men started rowing harder, all arguments between them forgotten. By now there were five pirate ships on our tail. Captain Gorgos ordered the sail turned and we changed direction, heading towards a small island on the horizon.

'That's Salamina,' said Peleas. 'It's heavily garrisoned with soldiers from the Greek army. We'll be safe if the wind holds and we make it into the harbour.'

Slowly, the distance between us and the pirate fleet widened. Soon we could see the entrance to the harbour on Salamina quite clearly. The pirates, guessing where Captain Gorgos was heading, fell away and headed back to the open sea. We were saved.

On Salamina, the crew offered sacrifice to Poseidon, pouring wine on the altar to show they were thankful he had saved us from the pirates. Captain Gorgos took the opportunity to have the water jars refilled and a priestess from the local temple reblessed our ship.

As we prepared to set sail again, the captain sacked the oarsman who'd lied about the mouse and we left him on the island. Thrax and I saw him standing stiffly on the quay as the remaining oarsmen carried us out of the harbour. He was glaring at us with eyes full of suppressed rage.

'That man looks positively evil,' shuddered Master Ariston dramatically, tossing crusts of stale bread to the dolphins in the water. 'I'm glad we've seen the last of him.'

The night passed without any more adventures and early the next morning we reached the port of Cenchreae near the Isthmus of Corinth. Our sailing across the Saronic Gulf was complete.

CHAPTER THREE

Under Attack

The Isthmus is a narrow land bridge that connects two parts of Greece, the north and the south. The city of Corinth lies at one end of it, overlooking the Ionian Sea, but we had docked at the other end, on the eastern side. A long journey on foot now lay ahead of us.

The noise in the harbour was deafening. Ships were unloading all kinds of cargo, from wine jars to large slabs of shining marble and planks of dried timber. Naval ships were moored to the quay, each one sporting a bronze ram at its prow.

'How will all these goods be taken to Corinth?' Thrax asked Captain Gorgos as we led Ariana braying down the gangplank.

'They will be carried across the Isthmus by cart or donkey,' explained the captain.

'There's a famous road called the Diolkos,' I added. 'It's paved with hard smooth stone so that sailors can drag a ship on rollers along it.'

'That's right,' agreed Captain Gorgos, watching Peleas and Tanoutamon load their crates of pottery on to a large donkey cart. 'It's far safer to drag a ship along the Diolkos than sail around the southern half of Greece. The gales around that stretch of coast can be deadly and some of the coves are infested with pirates.'

'Is the *Danais* going along the Diolkos?' asked Thrax.

'No,' said Captain Gorgos, 'I have cargo to pick up from the island of Crete. But I'll be back in Cenchreae to take you home after the wedding.'

He bid us goodbye, as did the archon, who was stopping at the port for a few days.

Master Ariston had thought of hiring a guide to take us to Corinth but it soon became clear that we did not need one. Dozens of people were making the same journey. We organised ourselves into a caravan and set off before the sun became too harsh for travel.

As we walked, we could hear sailors singing as they dragged their ship on rollers along the Diolkos.

'A ship across the land
Pulled by hand
Pulled by hand
A siren waiting in the sea
Just for me
Just for me
Will I ever get there?'

'That's a very good song,' said Master Ariston. 'Nico, make a note of it.' He scrambled on to Ariana and opened his cedar-wood box. Soon he was plucking the strings of his beloved lyre, singing to entertain our fellow travellers.

His unusually loud voice carried on the wind and other people in the caravan joined in. I could see Peleas further down the line singing along too. His slave Tanoutamon was walking silently beside him, stopping often to make sure the crates of pottery on the donkey cart were secure.

Around midday we stopped near an orchard to shelter from the heat and have a meal. We'd just refreshed ourselves at a stream and were ready to continue our journey when a scream rang out among the trees. Thrax looked up from the goatskin he was refilling.

'Master, I think we're under attack.'

He was right. Our caravan, laden with luxury goods for the people of Corinth, had attracted a band of thieves. Suddenly the air was full of hissing arrows, and pebbles from slings came whizzing past our heads. Peleas and Tanoutamon, who had joined us for lunch, both pulled out swords and disappeared into the jostling crowd. Thrax followed them, grabbing a fallen branch from the ground to use as a club. I wanted to go with him but Master Ariston held me back.

'Stay with me,' he said. 'I am carrying my jewellery under my himation.'

He spotted a small wayside shrine to Hera and we hid behind it, begging the almighty goddess to spare us. The sound of fighting stopped as suddenly as it had begun and Peleas returned, his chiton splattered with blood. My heart missed a beat when I did not see Thrax or Tanoutamon with him. Had they been injured or, worse, killed?

Thrax soon came running back to us with the club still in his hand. He had bad news. Tanoutamon had been felled by a sharp stone from a bandit's sling. It had struck him in the forehead.

Peleas went to retrieve the body and we buried it under the olive trees, marking the grave with a water jug Peleas took from his cargo.

'I thank the blessed Hera the rest of us escaped with no injury,' said Ariston. He turned to Peleas. 'Sell me a pot, sir. I shall leave it at her shrine as an offering.'

'All my large pieces are made to order,' replied Peleas. 'But I can spare you a small lekanis.'

He opened one of his baskets and drew out a small round pot. It was decorated with a scene showing the goddess Persephone leaving the underworld at the beginning of spring. Behind her, the mouth of the cave was full of shades, dead people cursed to wander in the dark forever.

Master Ariston placed it in the shrine, amongst other offerings of flowers and fruit that had withered and rotted with age.

'Won't bandits steal something so precious?' Thrax whispered to me as Master Ariston sang a hymn to the mother goddess.

'Not even bandits would dare remove offerings from a shrine,' I answered. 'Hera would strike them down.'

The hymn sung, we continued on our way to Corinth, each one of us lost in his own thoughts. The raid on the caravan had shaken me to the core. I'd never been caught up in such a savage attack before.

But sadness gave way to excitement as we approached Corinth. It was a clear night and the city's walls glowed like pure silver in the moonlight. Behind it on a steep hill stood a fort, also bathed in moonlight. The sound of sailors belting out rude songs in the harbour nearby carried on the breeze.

We passed under the flaming torches of the city gate and said goodbye to Peleas, who was lodging with a friend. Master Ariston asked the way to Zenon the Younger's residence and a small boy guided us to a house on a gentle slope above the agora.

Ahmose, Zenon's Egyptian slave and chief-of-staff, welcomed us with cups of wine, then showed us to our sleeping quarters. There was no place for Thrax and me in the slaves' main bedroom so Ahmose had set up two cots in the storeroom, a large hall packed to the ceiling with amphorae. It was damp and smelt strongly of stale wine but it was to become a very important place for secret meetings in the next few days and a sanctuary that I remember fondly.

CHAPTER FOUR

The Temple on the Hill

'That was a very eventful journey,' said Thrax after we'd stabled Ariana and were exploring Zenon's house. 'Sailors quarrelling over mice. Pirates chasing us across the sea. Bandits in the wilderness. The gruesome death of a trusted slave. You should write it all down, Nico, so we can read about it when we're old and our memories start to fade.'

I blinked at him in surprise. 'How do you mean?'

'I noticed you are very good with words,' replied Thrax. 'You should be doing something more interesting with your skills than taking down Master Ariston's rubbish.'

It had never occurred to me to write anything except what Master Ariston dictated but, now that Thrax had put the idea in my head, I was quite taken by it. All the people I admired were writers: playwrights, poets, historians... perhaps I too could become one of them.

But what sort of writing would I do? Sappho the poet was famous for her volumes of romantic lyrics, Herodotus for his fanciful accounts of historical events and famous people, Homer for epics that retold ancient myths. I needed to find a genre of writing that best suited my talents.

'Look at this kitchen,' said Thrax, interrupting my thoughts. 'It's got the biggest bread oven I've ever seen.'

Although the slaves' quarters in Master Zenon's house were cramped, the rest of the building was palatial. It had at least ten rooms that I could count, including a large hall – the andron – where Master Zenon entertained his friends. The women had a similar space – the gynaikeion – upstairs, where they spent most of the day spinning, weaving or sharing meals with close friends and relatives.

Behind the house was a narrow lane leading to a small farm and an orchard where Master Zenon's slaves grew vegetables, tended fruit trees and kept sheep and goats for milk. Here also were the stables where we'd left Ariana and a dovecote so lavish it looked like a small temple.

Master Ariston was given an airy room next to Master Zenon's, which he considered a great honour. He was quite impressed with the décor of the house, which was much grander and more colourful than we were used to in Athens.

'Father would call the style vulgar,' he said as we set out to explore Corinth the next morning. 'But I think it quite takes the breath away. You should see the bathroom, Nico. Such a huge bath, you can practically swim in it. And the mosaics!

There are mermaids and naked water nymphs all over the walls.'

Thrax and I had in fact already seen the bathroom. We had sneaked in during the night and cheekily given ourselves a good long wash and a rub down with perfumed oil. Rich masters might think slaves and badly paid scribes are not capable of appreciating the finer things in life but we are. It's just not in our interest to let them know about it.

Corinth was a bigger city than Athens, with smellier roads and much louder people. It had several temples, public baths, a theatre and the agora we'd seen the night before. These all lay in the shadow of the Acropolis high on the hill. Master Ariston told us locals called it the Acrocorinth. It had a famous temple of Aphrodite, whose beautiful priestesses were said to attract sailors from all over Hellas. Close to the temple was a sacred spring, which gushed out of the rocks into a large bathhouse. Legend told that Pegasus had created it by striking the bare rocks with his hooves.

'One hour in its pools is believed to give authors enough inspiration for a month,' Master Ariston informed us. 'I wish we had a magic spring like it back in Athens. I would bathe in it every day and write the most admired poems in the world.'

The city also had a paved road that led to a busy harbour. Here a weary traveller or sailor could revive himself drinking in one of the taverns that gave Corinth its reputation as livliest capital in the world.

Master Ariston dragged us up the hill to the Acrocorinth, as he wanted to bathe in the sacred spring at once. We were not the only people there taking the waters. A rather sickly looking man with straggly hair and blotchy skin was sitting in one of the pools, his long curly beard moving lazily with the current.

'I'm Euripides,' he introduced himself.

Master Ariston's leaned forward, his wet nostrils flaring with excitement. 'THE Euripides?'

'I am a well known writer of tragedies,' confirmed the man.

'I've seen several of your works,' gasped Master Ariston. 'And I was at the premiere of *Heracles* in Athens five years ago. You write

such strong roles for women, and such wisdom coming from the mouths of slaves.'

'I find slaves are often far more intelligent than their owners,' sniffed Euripides. 'I take it these are yours?'

'My father purchased Thrax for me at the market,' answered Ariston. 'He's the muscled one. The chubby lad is freeborn. His name's Nico.'

'Pleased to meet you, Thrax and Nico,' said Euripides, holding out a wet, wrinkled hand.

'Nico is my scribe,' went on Master Ariston.

Euripides nodded his head at me. 'Ah, so you're a writer too. A noble and divine profession, if I say so myself.'

'I agree,' declared Master Ariston loudly. 'I am an author as well.'

Euripides blew water out of his nose. 'How nice for you. What kind of author?'

'I write songs,' said Master Ariston. 'Which I perform at social functions in the manner of the great Arion.'

'Thank the gods you're not in the theatre,' replied Euripides. 'It's a cut-throat business,

I can tell you. Everyone wants to be a playwright these days.'

'The world of a travelling singer is gentler,' agreed Master Ariston. 'We're here to help the merchant Zenon celebrate his daughter's wedding. Will you be coming to one of his parties? Practically the whole of Corinth is invited.'

'I'm too busy to attend symposiums,' scoffed Euripides. 'A revival of *Alcestis* opens at the local theatre in nine days' time. We're re-staging it with major changes for the Corinthian audience. I was hoping to get the great Thespis for the main role but I'm afraid he's far too popular for our budget. Luckily, I have found a replacement with just as much talent if not fame. His name is Mikon and he plays women very convincingly. You should come and see him.'

'I'll get seats right away,' promised Master Ariston.

'Good!' The famous playwright closed his eyes and leaned back in the water.

'Come away, boys,' whispered Master Ariston dramatically as he filled a bottle with sacred water to take home with him. 'The great Euripides is resting. We mustn't disturb him any longer. Farewell, sir, pleased to have met you.'

Euripides opened one eye. 'Goodbye, boys. Do come and see me if you need anything while you're in Corinth. I am staying at the great inn by the harbour. The one with Pegasus painted above the door.'

'I can't believe we just met a famous playwright,' gushed Master Ariston as we made our way down the hill. 'What a gentleman.'

It seemed the bath in the sacred spring and the encounter with Euripides had worked wonders for Master Ariston's inspiration. The moment we were through the door, he asked me to fetch pen and ink.

'I shall compose a poem in honour of Corinth and my new friend Euripides,' he announced. 'Take this down, Nico, on the most luxurious papyrus we have, please. I'm sure the master playwright will want to see it the next time we meet him.'

CHAPTER FIVE

Trouble at the Party

Mistress Pandora's wedding was still a full ten days away but Master Zenon was already holding parties for his many male friends. These parties, or symposiums as Euripides the playwright had called them, were held in the andron. The guests reclined on soft couches while slaves served up delicious food and wine diluted with spring water. Sometimes there were jugglers or exotic dancers and Master Ariston was expected to perform at each of the parties.

My job in these gatherings was to sit discreetly behind him and write down any song or poem he made up on the spot. This happened quite often, although I suspect Master Ariston often cheated and composed the songs in his head beforehand. It made him very popular with the guests, though, who were always flattered that they had an inspired an artist.

Thrax attended the parties too, but mostly for show. He held the lyre when Master Ariston was not using it and mopped his master's brow when he perspired. This also happened often, and Master Ariston did not have to fake it. He was a very sweaty man. Still, he reckoned all that sweat pouring down his face made people see how hard poets have to work.

As father of the bride, Master Zenon hosted the parties while Ahmose was in charge of the food, the wine and the entertainment. It was clear by the way the guests at this first party talked about Master Zenon that he was very popular in Corinth. Thrax, however, insisted there must be a dark side to him. No one could get that rich without being ruthless.

We got proof of this dark side during the second party. Ahmose was serving a first course of iris bulbs marinated in vinegar when there was a loud crash upstairs. It was followed by the thud of footsteps running along a corridor. Then we heard two piercing screams, one louder than the other.

'What in the name of Zeus is going on up there?' growled Master Zenon, scowling at the ceiling.

Ahmose darted out of the andron and the guests looked at each other in alarm. Had fighting broken out among the slaves? Was the house under attack?

Ahmose returned with a grim expression on his face. 'Master, Mistress Pandora's loutrophoros has been smashed.'

A loutrophoros is a special wedding vase with a tall neck. It's a present from the groom to his bride. She uses it to pour the water for one last bath as a single woman before her wedding. Wealthy men compete with each other to buy the most expensive wedding vases and the best ones are imported from Athens.

Mistress Pandora's had been brought to Corinth by Peleas aboard the *Danais*. It had survived a journey across a pirate-infested sea and an ambush by fierce bandits. How strange to think that it now lay in pieces on the floor upstairs.

'Do you know who smashed it?' growled Master Zenon, a look of absolute fury showing in his eyes.

'The young slave Gaia was the only person in the room,' replied Ahmose. 'She must have knocked it over.'

'Forbid her to touch anything else in the house,' thundered Master Zenon. 'And send her to the slave market at the first opportunity. Tell Sosicles to order another wedding vase for his bride. I shall not have my daughter getting married without the proper ceremonies.'

'Yes, master.' Ahmose bowed and hurried out of the room once more. Master Ariston began singing again but the mood in the room had changed. The incident had obviously caused Master Zenon a lot of embarrassment. Rich men

like him are meant to have the best slaves in the city, not careless ones who destroy priceless treasures.

Thrax was shaking with anger when we went to bed that night. But it wasn't the broken wedding vase that had upset him. 'Did you hear Master Zenon?' he fumed. 'A poor girl breaks a piece of pottery and she's packed off to the slave market without a second thought. There's no attempt to find out if it was an accident, or if somebody else smashed the vase. I tell you, Nico, there's no justice in this world if you're a slave.'

CHAPTER SIX

An Offer of Gold

The next morning dawned grey and misty, which was unusual for spring in Corinth. Master Ariston woke up late in a foul mood. The disaster at last night's party had spoiled his creative flow. How could he write romantic poems when all people wanted to talk about was a smashed wedding vase?

'I'm going to the barber to have my hair trimmed,' he said, pushing away his breakfast of bread and wine. 'And then I am going to the sacred spring for inspiration. Neither of you need come with me. I'm taking Ariana. I want total solitude until the muse returns. Thrax, fetch me my himation.'

He popped a few small coins in the side of his mouth in case he wanted to buy refreshments, and left. Thrax and I wolfed down the remains of his breakfast.

'I'm still hungry,' said Thrax, rinsing the breakfast bowl at the well in the yard. 'Staring at all that delicious party food yesterday has given me a giant's appetite.'

'Let's beg some fruit from the cook,' I suggested. 'I met her yesterday and she looked quite friendly.'

We wandered into the kitchen, a long, low-ceilinged room to one side of the yard. There was a large blackened pot simmering under a hole in the roof for the smoke and next to it a copper brazier used for making breakfast pancakes. A heap of freshly picked beans lay on a table waiting to be podded but Cook was nowhere to be seen. I noticed two large wicker baskets in a corner. Both were filled with loaves of freshly baked bread.

'Don't touch them,' said Thrax. 'And let's get out before someone sees us. If we're accused of stealing you might end up in exile and I'd be pushed to my death off the Acrocorinth.'

We were about to leave when a scraping sound stopped us dead in our tracks. One of the bread baskets in the corner wobbled and moved sideways. A hooded figure in a dark himation rose up behind it. It extended a finger towards us and hissed. 'Come, follow me.'

Looking closer, I noticed the figure had emerged from a dark hole in the wall. The wicker basket had been hiding the entrance to a secret passage!

'I've been waiting here for ages, hoping you'd come to the kitchen,' whispered the dark shape again. 'I beg you, come with me. We haven't much time before Cook returns from the fish market. It's a matter of life and death.'

The figure ducked back into the passage and we followed. 'Push the bread basket back in place and close the door behind you,' the figure hissed at Thrax, who was bringing up the rear. 'I don't want Cook to discover the secret passage.'

Thrax did as we were asked.

'Don't be scared,' continued the figure, taking down a flickering lamp from a ledge in the tunnel. 'We'll be out of here in no time.'

'Neither of us is scared, ma'am,' said Thrax.

Ma'am? Trust Thrax to have noticed that the mysterious figure in the swirling cloak was high-born. I hadn't even noticed it was a girl.

We came to a wooden ladder and the girl handed me the lamp. 'Hold this, please.'

She clambered up the rungs and a moment later, pale light flooded down into the passage. The mysterious girl had opened another door. Thrax and I followed her, stepping out into a fragrant-smelling room.

The girl threw back her himation to release a cascade of dark curly hair. She was very pretty, with large green eyes and a gold necklace around her neck.

'That secret passage is very handy,' she said as she closed the door behind us and dragged a chest to hide it. 'It was built a long time ago so that the women in the house could escape during pirate raids. Now Corinth is so powerful the pirates don't raid our houses any more and the passage has been forgotten. Welcome to the women's quarters.'

The room we were in was much more lavishly decorated than any I had seen before. The walls were a soft pink, with a pattern of scalloped seashells painted in a border just below the ceiling.

A chair and table sat in a corner, both beautifully carved and painted a bright blue. Next to them was a second chest with a metal lock shaped like a Medusa's head. Tucked under a window on the other side of the room was a single bed with soft pillows.

'You have a very nice bedroom, ma'am,' said Thrax, 'but if my friend and I are caught in here we'll be in serious trouble.'

'Don't worry,' replied the girl. 'There's no one about. Father and Ahmose are offering sacrifice at the temple and I sent Nanny out to look for wild cherries. I insisted she get me a whole basketful so she won't be back for a while. My mother and sister are weaving on the other side of the house.'

She held out her hand in greeting as if she were a boy. 'My name is Fotini. I am the bride's younger sister.'

'We're both pleased to meet you,' said Thrax, shaking her hand. 'But why have you brought us here?'

'I need your help,' replied Mistress Fotini. 'Please wait a moment.' She shut the window, then pulled up two stools to the bed and reclined on the pillows. 'Sit, both of you. As you know, my slave girl Gaia was accused of smashing my sister's wedding vase last night. My father was very embarrassed by the incident so he's decided to sell her. Gaia has been my personal slave ever since I can remember and I want her to stay. She's like a sister to me.'

'Do you think she is to blame?' I asked.

'The loutrophoros was in my sister's room,' said Mistress Fotini. 'Gaia was in there when the accident happened but she swears she didn't break it. The girl can be a bit of a dreamer but I believe her.'

'With all due respect,' said Thrax, 'I don't see what this has got to do with Nico and me.'

'I eavesdropped on my father having lunch with the poet yesterday,' said Mistress Fotini. 'Your master described how you settled an argument between the rowers on board the *Danais*. It seems you have a talent for solving mysteries. Will you find out who really smashed the vase?'

'It's not wise for a slave to get involved in a dispute between freemen,' replied Thrax.

'Please,' said Mistress Fotini gently. 'Think about it before you refuse me. If you do find the culprit, I will pay you... in gold.'

CHAPTER SEVEN

Enter the Cyclops

'You must take on the case,' I said to Thrax as we slipped out of the kitchen. Mistress Fotini had let us out of her room through the secret passage, reminding us to put the bread basket back in place.

Thrax looked at me defiantly. 'Why should I? Mistress Fotini can get another slave to do her bidding.'

I filled a cup of water for both of us and we took them out to the yard. 'I heard you talking in your sleep back home in Athens. You said you wanted to find your mother in Thrace when you have enough money. Well, now's your chance. Mistress Fotini said she'd pay you in gold. With your keen eye for detail and your intelligence, you'll have the reward under your belt in no time. And you could go on solving mysteries for other people until you have all the money you need. Before you know it, you'll be rich and free.'

'I don't need help from wealthy slave owners,' snapped Thrax. 'I'll find another way to make money.'

'How?' I said. 'By becoming a thief yourself? Slaves don't get that many opportunities to gain riches. Besides, you wouldn't just be helping Mistress Fotini, you'd be saving Gaia too. Remember how angry you were when Master Zenon said he was going to sell her?'

Thrax didn't reply. A faraway look came into his eyes and I knew he was thinking hard. We sat in the shade of a vine and I sipped the cool water. The sun rose higher in the sky, poking its hot rays through the vine, but I didn't dare move. I didn't want to disturb Thrax while he was thinking.

Above me the swallows twittered as they darted in out of the holes in the courtyard walls and the doves cooed on the windowsills.

At last Thrax opened his eyes again.

'You're right, Nico,' he said, 'this might be my only chance to make some money and buy freedom for my mother and myself. I'll take on the case – on two conditions.'

I looked at him, puzzled. 'What?'

'The first is that you'll be my assistant,' said Thrax. 'I'm going to need a lot of help if I'm to solve this mystery. The second is that you write about the case. If I have a talent for solving problems, you have one for writing.'

Write about solving mysteries! Now why hadn't I thought of that? I was pretty sure no author in Hellas was writing mystery stories. This could be the perfect opportunity for me to make my mark in the world of storytelling.

'By the writing hand of Cadmus, it's a deal,' I said. We shook hands to seal the agreement and Thrax suggested we beg some cooking wine off Cook to celebrate.

She'd just come back from the market with the shopping, a short woman, round as a water jug with dark hair cropped close to her head. She spoke with a strange accent, which Thrax said marked her out as a woman from Phrygia, a land to the east of Hellas. One of his friends at the farm near Thebes had also come from the same country. She gave us not only wine but hunks of stale cake to dip in it too.

'There's no symposium tonight,' she said as we helped her put away the shopping. 'Master Zenon is taking part in a secret ceremony out in the woods. He's invited your master to go along with him. It's a very hush-hush ceremony for rich men only. No boys allowed. All slaves in the house have the night off so there's only the three of us for supper tonight. I'll make a special treat from back home. Rabbit stew with beans.'

She poked me gently in the tummy and laughed. 'You look like you enjoy your food and your friend here needs more of it to keep his muscles big and strong.'

I was delighted to hear we were in for a lavish banquet, and that the house would be almost deserted. It gave Thrax and me the chance to let Mistress Fotini know he was taking on the case.

Master Ariston came back from the sacred spring, wanting to be pampered and perfumed. For the next few hours Thrax was kept busy heating water, scrubbing his spotty back and rubbing him down with perfumed oil till he smelt like cherry blossom. When, at last, both masters were ready to leave, Ahmose brought round a horse-drawn carriage and they disappeared down the scrubby road.

We had our dinner out in the courtyard, with Cook refilling our bowls the moment we emptied them. The stars were twinkling in the sky by the time we finished the meal and Cook belched loudly. Thrax offered to wash the dishes and she retired to bed in a small chamber off the kitchen.

When we could hear her snoring, I pushed aside the bread basket and we crept into the secret passage. A few minutes later we had scaled the ladder and I rapped on the secret door.

Mistress Fotini answered it. 'Welcome back,' she whispered. 'But I'm afraid we'll have to be quiet. Pandora is sleeping in the room next door.' She lit a small lamp and placed it carefully on a three-legged table.

'Nico's convinced me to take on the case,' said Thrax, settling on the stool he'd sat on earlier, 'but I need to convince myself that Gaia is innocent. When can I speak to her?'

'Right now,' replied Mistress Fotini. She went to the chest with the Medusa lock and carefully pulled it open. There was a rustle of linen as a little girl stood up. She peered around the room with big frightened eyes.

'These boys are friends,' said Mistress Fotini gently. 'They're going to prove that you didn't break Mistress Pandora's wedding vase.'

Gaia stepped out of the chest shyly, watching Thrax and I as if we were foxes about to pounce on a duckling. She looked younger than her mistress by a couple of years, with skin that glowed almost like glass in the lamplight. I guessed she was Syrian or perhaps Egyptian like Ahmose.

'This boy wants to ask you some questions,' Mistress Fotini explained. 'His name is Thrax. And his friend here is Nico.'

Gaia looked from me to Thrax then lowered her gaze to the floor. 'I promise I didn't smash Mistress Pandora's wedding vase, sir,' she said softly.

'You don't need to call me "sir",' said Thrax. 'I am a slave like you. Now tell me what happened.'

'It was starting to get dark,' began Gaia. 'Mistress Pandora ordered me to light the lamps in her room.'

'Why did Mistress Pandora ask you to do that?' asked Thrax. 'Doesn't she have a personal slave of her own?'

'Yes, her name is Kaliope,' said Gaia. 'But she was taking a long time choosing a necklace.'

'We invited a Persian merchant woman to come and show us her jewellery,' explained Mistress Fotini. 'She specialises in ornaments for weddings. Father said even the slaves are to have necklaces for the wedding. We were all in the

74

gynaikeion choosing pieces when the accident happened.'

Thrax smiled at Gaia. 'So you'd chosen your own necklace for the wedding and Mistress Pandora sent you to light the lamps in her room. Was the window open when you went in?'

'Yes.'

'As you know it was hot last night,' said Mistress Fotini. 'We had the windows in the women's quarters wide open to let in the breeze.'

'And we wanted to hear the sound of the party downstairs,' added Gaia.

'Was there anyone in the room when you went in?' asked Thrax.

Gaia shook her head. 'No one.'

'And where was the vase?'

'It was on the linen chest in the corner. I didn't need to get close to see how beautiful it was. The moonlight from the window made it glow so brightly I could see the picture on it from across the room. It was such a pretty picture. There was a wedding cart with horses taking the bride to her new home. She looked just like Mistress Pandora. A groom was driving the cart. He was as handsome as I imagine Prince Theseus was. And there were children in the picture too, waving and cheering. It must be very exciting riding on a wedding cart to your new home. I want to be a bride one day.'

'Did you not wonder if there might be something inside the vase?' asked Thrax. 'I'm always tempted to look inside a pot in case there's something in it.'

'Gaia knew the vase was empty,' Mistress Fotini put in. 'We both watched Mother unpack it.'

Thrax nodded and turned to Gaia again. 'So you were standing across the room in the dark, dreaming of the day when you too will be a happy bride. What happened next?'

'I heard a grunt,' said Gaia. 'I looked round and there was a horrible-looking man climbing through the window. He didn't see me because I was standing in the dark. But I saw *him*. Ugh! He smelt like an open tomb when we go to pay our respects at the graveyard.'

'Why didn't you scream when you saw him?' asked Thrax.

Gaia's eyes filled with tears. 'I tried, but no sound came out of my mouth.'

'That does tend to happen when we get very scared,' said Thrax gently. 'What did you do next?'

'Nothing,' said Gaia. 'I was so terrified I felt as if I'd turned into a statue. The thief picked up the wedding vase and I think it slipped out of his hands. I couldn't see properly because he had his back to me. The crash was so loud it made him jump. Then he grabbed one of the pieces of broken pottery and disappeared out of the window. Kaliope ran into the room a few moments later. She screamed when she saw the broken vase and that made me scream too. Then Mistress Pandora came running down the corridor. I told her about the thief smashing the vase but when we looked out of the window there was no one in the lane. So I got blamed and now I must be sold.'

'Father won't sell you, I promise,' Mistress Fotini comforted her, squeezing Gaia's hand and giving her a honey cake from a small dish. 'I won't let him do it.'

She turned to Thrax. 'I'll take her to the temple of Aphrodite tomorrow. The priestesses will give her sanctuary until you catch the thief. I donate a lot of money to the temple because I'm going to be a priestess myself when I grow up. They wouldn't dare refuse me.'

'Was there anything else in the room that the burglar might have been tempted to steal?' asked Thrax.

'Yes,' Mistress Fotini answered for her slave. 'Jewellery and some money. But the thief didn't notice them. He must have panicked when he smashed the vase.'

'Did you get a good look at the thief's face?' Thrax asked Gaia. 'If you saw him again, would you recognise him?'

'Oh yes,' replied Gaia without hesitation. 'He had a terrible face with only one eye. He was a Cyclops.'

There was silence in the room as we all thought about Gaia's statement.

'Seeing a Cyclops can be terrifying,' said Thrax at last.

'And she did notice some other things about him,' Mistress Fotini nudged Gaia. 'Go on, tell Thrax and Nico.'

'He was really huge and tall,' whispered Gaia. 'And I noticed his arms when he reached for the vase. They were covered in horrible scars.'

'You've had a horrible experience,' said Thrax. 'But don't be scared any more. Nico and I are going to find him and bring him to justice. Have you told this to anyone else?'

Gaia hung her head. 'Only Master Zenon, and he doesn't believe me. He thinks I've made the story up.'

Thrax turned to Mistress Fotini. 'You must take her to the temple at once. We'll be in touch again soon. Goodnight.'

Mistress Fotini let us out of her room and we stole back to our sleeping corner in the storeroom. The house was still silent. The male slaves had not yet come back from their night in town.

I fetched a snack of walnuts and raisins to help us think while Thrax lit a lamp.

And then we had our first ever secret meeting. How were we to go about tracking down the thief?

CHAPTER EIGHT

Our First Secret Meeting

'I'll take notes,' I said to Thrax. 'Writing things down always help me sort them out in my head.'

I fished out my wax tablet, which I always keep under my bed along with a stylus. 'Are you sure Gaia didn't smash the vase and make up the story about the Cyclops? I have to admit, it does sound a bit fanciful.'

'I am certain she's innocent,' replied Thrax.

'Why?'

'She hasn't the imagination to make up a story about a Cyclops. She's telling the truth.'

'But it couldn't have been a real Cyclops. There's no such thing. It must have been a man in a mask.'

'Perhaps,' said Thrax.

'I wish we could inspect Mistress Pandora's room. The thief might have left some clues.'

'There'd be no footprints,' Thrax assured me. 'It hasn't rained recently so the ground would be too dry for mud. And even if the Cyclops did leave any traces of his visit, the slaves would have cleaned them away by now. They scrub the rooms every morning.'

'That leaves us very little to go on. If only the thief were a real Cyclops. It would be very easy to find a one-eyed man, even in a city as big as Corinth.'

'But Gaia gave us some very strong clues,' said Thrax. 'Four, to be precise. They're enough to unmask the thief and bring him to justice.'

I thought back to our conversation with Gaia.

'She said the thief smelt like a corpse,' I said.
'I'll write that down. It sounds important.'

I scratched SMELLS LIKE A CORPSE in the wax tablet.

'She didn't say "corpse",' Thrax corrected me. 'She said "like an open grave". There's a big difference.'

I scratched out CORPSE and wrote LIKE AN OPEN GRAVE.

'What does an open grave smell like?' said Thrax.

'Damp,' I replied. 'Musty.'

Thrax nodded. 'And what kind of person would smell musty?'

'Someone who works with damp earth. A brick maker who makes mud bricks, perhaps. Or a gravedigger.'

'And then there are the scars,' continued Thrax. 'Clue number two. What kind of person would have lots of scars all over their arms?'

'Someone who sharpens knives and tools for a living?'

'I used to help Cook on the farm bake bread,' said Thrax. 'Often, when she reached into the hot oven for a loaf, she'd accidentally brush her arm against the edge of the oven door. The hot clay left burn marks on her forearm that turned into scars. Her right arm was laddered with them.'

'So are we looking for a baker?' I wondered.

'Bakers smell of baked bread or fermenting yeast,' said Thrax. 'This one reeks of damp earth. I reckon it's clay – that smells musty. The thief must handle clay so much it leaves a smell on his skin and clothes. And he works with an oven. An oven that has clay objects in it – a potter's kiln!'

I'd never thought of jugs and vases going into an oven, but in fact they're baked, or 'fired' to harden the clay.

'So are we looking for a potter?' I asked.

'We're looking for a potter's assistant,' said Thrax. 'Most likely a slave. It's the assistant's job to put the pots in the kiln and pull them out again when they're fired.'

'But if the thief works for a potter, why did he break into a house to steal a wedding vase? Why not just steal one from his own place of work? Wouldn't that be easier?'

'Stealing from his own place of work would be too risky. He'd be the first suspect,' said Thrax.

'I wonder how the thief knew there would be a wedding vase in Master Zenon's house?' I said.

'Peleas the merchant must have a local agent. The agent takes orders from rich clients in Corinth, and Peleas supplies the vases from Athens. The thief might work with the agent and have heard about the wedding vase. He might even have planned the theft before the vase reached Corinth.'

I wrote the rest of the clues in my tablet before showing it to Thrax. 'So we are looking for a thief who 1) is a potter's assistant, 2) is tall and hulking, 3) smells of wet clay and 4) has distinctive scars all over his arm, most likely the right one. Those are the four clues Gaia gave us. But how do we go about finding a potter's assistant in one of the biggest cities in the world? It's like looking for a drop in the ocean.'

'The man probably works for Peleas's agent,' Thrax reminded me. 'The first thing to do is find out who that is...'

Suddenly he stopped talking and looked around the room. 'Shh...' he whispered, putting a finger to his lips. He tiptoed to the door and yanked it open. But there was no one outside, and after peering out into the yard, he closed it again.

'I thought I heard someone outside the room. We're going to have to be very careful when we discuss the case. There's also the possibility that someone in this house might be in league with the thief.'

Just then we heard banging at the front door. The other slaves had come back from their night out. I slipped the wax tablet under my bed. Our first secret meeting was over.

CHAPTER NINE

Enquiries at the Market

Two whole frustrating days went by before Thrax and I could start trying to find Peleas's agent. The great wedding was now almost upon us and Master Ariston kept us both busy, me copying down new songs and Thrax cleaning his clothes and making snacks to help with the inspiration.

Zenon's house was frantic with activity. Cook baked almond cakes all day long, singing at the top of her lungs as she stirred the batter or threw logs into the oven. Ahmose organised the slaves into a cleaning party. The male slaves were set repainting the yard, scrubbing the altar and hanging a huge awning to cast shade across the yard. Every wooden chest and piece of furniture in the house was oiled until it shone like a mirror. Even the farm and the stables got a tidy-up.

The women swept every room and washed the linen curtains in vinegar to whiten them. Master Ariston found it very difficult to work with all the noise and mess. 'I can't hear myself think,' he complained after two days of whirling dust and clanging bronze buckets. 'I need to compose a celebration piece in honour of the groom's father. I've been told he breeds dogs. How can I write about dogs when all I seem to hear is pigeons cooing?'

'Ahmose is repainting the dovecote, sir,' I said. 'The pigeons have fled to the windowsills in the courtyard.'

'I don't blame them,' said Master Ariston. 'The smell of that paint is strong enough to kill a sacred bull. I'm sure it's affecting my throat.'

He called for Thrax. 'Get Cook to make me a soothing tonic with hot water and honey.'

'You should gargle with some tea made with herbs of Cilicia too, master,' said Thrax, winking at me. 'It works wonders on a sore throat. I can get you some from the market right now.'

'Now that's a good idea,' said Master Ariston. 'You do look after me well, Thrax.'

'I'll go with him, sir,' I cut in. 'We're running low on papyrus and you need spare strings for your lyre.'

'Very well,' said Master Ariston, tossing a clinking purse at me. 'I'm going to work in the temple of Aphrodite. Hopefully it'll be nice and quiet at the sacred spring. I'll take a wax tablet and write down the lyrics myself. You don't need to hurry back. I'll be busy all day.'

Thrax fetched him the tonic and we left him sipping it noisily. It was still mid-morning. The city was buzzing with activity and I was thrilled we were starting our investigations at last.

'Your little trick to get us out of the house worked perfectly,' I said to Thrax as we made our way down the hill. 'We might even get lucky and spot the thief himself. We're looking for a tall, hulking man with scars all over his right arm. It shouldn't be too difficult to spot him if he's there.'

'He'll be a dangerous fellow,' said Thrax, 'so if we do see him, we'll have to be careful he doesn't see *us*.'

I walked quickly to keep up with my friend who always had a steady pace. 'Perhaps it's safer to find out if he works with Peleas's agent. But even if we find him, how are we going to prove he smashed Mistress Pandora's vase? Remember, he left no clues in the room.'

Thrax didn't answer. I was beginning to realise that he never revealed his thoughts until they were perfectly clear in his mind.

We found the agora teeming with people, like an anthill at the height of summer. There were stalls laden with fish, still gasping from being pulled out of the sea. Others boasted ripe vegetables and fruit, or cloth in every colour of the rainbow. Hawkers thrust pots of perfume at us, waving them under our noses. 'Best balm of

Egypt! Bark essence to soothe an itchy skin!'

Children shouted out the prices of puppies and goslings.

We spied cheap jewellery and statues of gods, and blue amulets shaped like eyes to ward off sickness and bad luck. I found the stall selling papyrus and stopped to admire it. It had lots of other wonderful things for sale too. Reed pens and styluses, and inkwells in various shapes and sizes, some of them with cork stoppers to stop the ink drying up.

'Look at these little knives,' said Thrax. 'They have beautiful bone handles.'

'They're sharpening knives. Scribes use them on their kalamos.'

While I haggled with the stallholder over the price of the papyrus, Thrax went off in search of the herbs of Cilicia. When he returned, his eyes were bright with excitement.

'I've found the pottery section,' he said. 'It's right at the end of the market behind the fountains. Let's see if anyone there can tell us who Peleas's agent in Corinth is.'

We approached the stalls, which were laden with pots of all shapes and sizes. 'There's something here for every occasion,' said Thrax, stopping at one of them.

'What can I get you, boys?' asked a stallholder, a very thin man with unusually blue eyes. 'A nice alabastron for your girlfriends, perhaps?' He looked at my ink-stained fingers. 'Or how about a nice inkwell for the discerning scribe? Lots of them going cheap today.'

He nodded at some wicker baskets placed in front of the stall to tempt buyers.

'We're not shopping today,' replied Thrax. 'My friend the scribe here is writing a song about a wedding vase and we wondered what a really expensive one would look like.'

'You won't find any wedding vases worth writing about in the agora,' laughed the stallholder. 'Most traders here only stock pots for working people.'

'We were hoping to see a vase as grand as one you might buy from Peleas of Athens,' said Thrax.

'You'd have to visit Peleas' agent to see one of those.' The stallholder started pulling down the shutters. 'That's Alcandros the Elder. Peleas stays with him when he's in Corinth but someone told me they saw them leaving the city three days ago.'

'Then how will we be able to see one of Peleas's grand vases?' said Thrax.

The stallholder laughed. 'I'm sure whoever Alcandros left in charge of his warehouse would show you one if you asked politely.'

'But where would we find Alcandros's warehouse?' I asked.

The stallholder slammed down the last shutter and took a rusty key from a chain hanging at his belt. 'In the potters' district, where else?'

'We're new to Corinth,' said Thrax. 'Can you tell us how to get there?'

'Go out of the agora by the western gate,' replied the stallholder, 'then follow the main street till you come to a small ruined temple. Turn left at the temple and you'll see the pottery workshops and warehouses tucked under the city walls. Anyone there will show you which one belongs to Alcandros, although I should imagine it'll be closed for the afternoon.'

We thanked the stallholder and made our way out of the agora. With a few hours to kill before Alcandros's warehouse opened again, I reckoned we had time for lunch and bought some fried parrotfish in bread. We ate it sitting in the shade of an olive tree. There seemed to be no one about except us.

'Peleas must have gone to Athens to get a new loutrophoros for Mistress Pandora,' I said as I gobbled up the last piece of fish. 'And Alcandros went with him for protection now that his slave Tanoutamon is dead.'

Thrax finished his lunch too. 'Perhaps! Although Alcandros might just have gone to see what new styles are coming out of Athenian potteries.'

After our meal we stretched out on the grass and had a long nap. When we woke up again, the city was coming back to life. We washed our faces at a spring and followed the stallholder's directions to the potters' district.

CHAPTER TEN
An Ode to a Vase

The ruined temple soon loomed up before us. Turning left as we'd been told, we saw the potters' district right ahead. It was a jumble of busy workshops and warehouses, all painted a bright terracotta colour. The narrow streets were packed with people carrying enormous pots on their backs or loading carts with vases and storage jars.

Potters sat at their wheels outside every workshop, their hands magically turning lumps of wet clay into smooth round bowls or jugs. The doors to the shops were wide open and we caught tantalising glimpses of beautiful pots inside.

A small girl tugged at my tunic and held out a handful of clay amulets on strings. They were little round medallions with badly carved Medusas on them.

'Very pretty,' she said in a voice so soft I could hardly hear her. 'Medusa keeps away bad luck. We have a special offer today. Four lucky charms for the price of one.'

She looked so hopeful, I couldn't help fishing a coin out of my bag. The girl smiled and handed me four amulets. She giggled shyly when Thrax went down on one knee so she could slip the medallion over his head.

'Thank you,' he said. 'We are looking for Alcandros the potter. Can you tell us where his warehouse is?'

The girl nodded and led us to a large doorway further down the street. It had a clean white linen curtain across it and a large plaque showing Athena with an owl on her shoulder. Thrax parted the curtain and we stepped into cool shade. A dog immediately leaped up behind a wooden counter and started howling ferociously.

'Be quiet, Cerberus,' hissed a voice further inside the shop. We heard light footsteps and a man appeared from behind a shelf full of vases. He had even bigger muscles than Thrax, and his head was shaved too. 'Don't be scared of Cerberus,' he said, patting the dog gently. 'His bark is worse than his bite. What can I do for you, boys?'

'We'd like to see an Athenian vase,' said Thrax. 'My friend here is a writer, trying to compose an ode to a vase. We were told at the agora that Alcandros might let us have a look at some of his fine pots.'

'Master Alcandros is away on urgent business,' said the man behind the counter. 'He won't be back for a few days but I'm sure he won't mind me showing you some of our best vases. I'm Donos and I'm in charge when the boss is away.' He shook our hands and I noticed right away that his arms were covered in scars. He was too short to be our thief though, and he smelt of perfumed oil, not damp clay. 'Let me fetch a piece I think might inspire you.'

The moment he disappeared among the shelves, Thrax and I started to take a good look around us. There were stacks of expensive pottery all over the place but no sign of a second assistant. Nor could we hear the sound of anyone working a potter's wheel out the back. The only noise was Cerberus growling softly behind the counter.

'Does Master Alcandros make his own vases here?' asked Thrax when Donos returned with a stamnos and placed it on the counter.

'He does,' said Donos. 'But he also imports vases from all over the world; Athens, Thrace, Illyria, Egypt, even from Samos. And I throw pots too. I even paint them myself.' He indicated the stamnos. 'This is my latest piece.'

We stared at the beautiful work of art in front of us. It showed a picture of Zeus sharing a cup of wine with Dionysus. Behind them was a temple with Corinthian columns, full of cats and foxes with bushy tails, both animals said to be dear to the wine god. Above the temple, rain clouds were gathering. They were painted to suggest luxurious curtains, like you might find at the door of a palace.

'I'm amazed you find the time to create such detailed pieces,' said Thrax. 'You must be run off your feet looking after this place. Do you not have any help?'

'I'm the only one here besides Master Alcandros,' replied Donos. 'I have to light up the kiln, fire the pottery and look after customers too.'

'Your vases are stunning,' I said. 'You must charge a fortune for them.'

The pride on Donos's face was replaced by a sad look. 'Master Alcandros does ask a lot for my work,' he said, 'but he only pays me an obol for every piece.'

'You'd be lucky to get a loaf of bread for that,' said Thrax. 'The gods are harsh.'

The sad look in Donos's eyes changed into one of defiance and his hands gripped the vase. 'But I will be a free man one day. Then I'll set up my own workshop in Athens and make pots fit for kings.'

Cerberus reared up behind the counter and started barking madly. The angry look on

Donos's face was immediately replaced with a professional smile. 'Well, I think there are some customers coming. It's been nice talking to you, boys. Do come and see me again.'

He shook my hand. 'Good luck with your poem. I hope my work has inspired you. Come and show it to me when it's finished.'

We left the shop as an old man and his slave, both richly dressed, came in through the linen curtain. The little girl with the lucky charms waved to us from across the street.

'Donos works on his own,' I said to Thrax as we walked back towards the ruined temple.

'That means the thief must have heard about Pandora's wedding vase from another source,' he replied. 'We need to widen our search but we'll get him in the end, I promise.' He walked faster. 'Let's get home before Master Ariston. He'll be in a bad mood all evening if I'm not there to give him the herbs of Cilicia.'

But even though we hurried, Master Ariston got home before us. He was sitting at the table with Cook as we stumbled through the kitchen door, our eyes hurting from the bright sunlight.

His throat seemed to be completely healed. 'You won't believe it,' he roared through a mouthful of cheese and grapes. 'A thief broke into the temple of Aphrodite this afternoon and tried to steal an oinoche. They'd only had the jug in the temple a few days.'

'I went up to the Acrocorinth for some inspiring peace and quiet and all I got was a brood of priestesses screaming and running about like hens chased by a fox. Cook tells me Mistress Fotini was there too. Fancy a thief breaking into a sacred temple. He didn't manage to get away with the oinoche, though. He dropped it and it smashed to pieces on the steps outside the temple. Can you believe it?'

CHAPTER ELEVEN

In the Women's Quarters

'Is Corinth infested with clumsy thieves or is it the same person?' I asked Thrax as we scrubbed the city dust from our faces.

'It's impossible to tell without more information. We need to talk to Mistress Fotini. Perhaps she saw something.'

Once again Master Zenon was not holding a symposium for his friends that night. It was the women's turn to celebrate. Mistress Pandora was offering sacrifice to the mother goddess at the household altar. A large crowd of aunts, cousins and close female friends had come to take part in the celebration and the house was full of their chatter and laughter. Cook had made special griddled cakes in her copper brazier and slaves were running from door to door upstairs, handing them out.

We men were not allowed to watch the ceremony so Thrax and I accompanied Master Ariston to the harbour for a meal. It was well past midnight when we returned to the house and the guests had left. The only sound we could hear was Ahmose praying loudly to Isis in his room.

We waited patiently until his chanting turned to snoring, then slipped past Cook's chamber into the passage behind the bread basket in the kitchen. We climbed up the ladder and Thrax knocked lightly on the secret door.

Mistress Fotini answered it immediately. 'Welcome,' she whispered. 'We'll have to be careful again tonight. Some of the guests are staying here until the wedding. They're asleep on cots in my mother's chamber and the gynaikeion.'

She offered us some cakes left over from the party and poured honeyed water into small cups. Thrax nodded at me to start taking notes.

'We hear someone tried to steal an oinoche from the temple,' he said to Mistress Fotini. 'Did anyone manage to get a good look at the thief? Was he wearing a Cyclops mask?'

'Only Sister Agatha saw him,' replied Mistress Fotini, 'and she only got a fleeting glimpse. She said she saw the back of a shadowy figure, and just for a moment or two. Not long enough to notice if he was wearing a mask or to identify him if she saw him again. Sister Agatha is a very old woman and her eyesight is failing. It's also very dark in the temple. The only light is supposed to come from a flame burning in front of the goddess but that had gone out.'

'Perhaps the thief put it out,' I suggested.

'Probably,' agreed Mistress Fotini. 'It's a great insult to the goddess. We'll have to have a special ceremony to light a new flame.'

I wrote THIEF IN TEMPLE NOT IDENTIFIED. MASK OR NOT? on my wax tablet.

'Was Sister Agatha completely alone when the thief struck?' asked Thrax. 'Are you sure there was no one else with her?'

'I'm sure she was alone,' said Mistress Fotini. 'She was placing an offering at the feet of the goddess. The rest of us were having a meal in the priestesses' house. Gaia was with me so this time no one can say she had anything to do with it.'

'What time of day did the incident happen?'

'Late afternoon. I know because that's when sailors come up from the harbour hoping to catch a glimpse of the priestesses.'

'Are offerings normally placed in front of the goddess in the afternoon?'

Mistress Fotini shook her head. 'No, this was a rare occasion. The priestesses usually go into the temple much later, after the evening star is seen in the heavens. But yesterday a woman came with an offering of pomegranates. Her husband was sailing to Egypt at sunset and she wanted to make sure the goddess would protect him during the voyage. She insisted that the offering be placed in front of the goddess before her husband's ship left the harbour.'

'I see,' said Thrax. 'I take it the door to the treasure house is directly behind the goddess as in all other temples.'

'Yes. It's locked with a key which the high priestess keeps on a chain round her waist.'

I scribbled KEY NOT AVAILABLE TO THIEF on my wax tablet.

'The thief would have picked the lock,' said Thrax, and I hastily erased my last note. 'How were you alerted to the crime?'

'Sister Agatha let out a piercing scream. She heard the rustle of the curtain at the door and looked up from putting down the offering just in time to see a figure silhouetted in the doorway. We all went running but by the time we reached the temple the thief had vanished into thin air.'

'And you are absolutely sure he only took the jug?' said Thrax.

'Yes. The high priestess made a very careful check of the treasury after the burglary. Nothing else was touched. But it's a shame the oinoche was smashed. It was a beautiful work of art, hand-painted in Athens. The high priestess bought it for the goddess herself.'

'Could there have been something inside the jug that the thief might have wanted?' asked Thrax.

'No. An oinoche is filled with sacred water, oil or wine during a ritual. Nothing else is ever placed inside it.'

Thrax stood up to leave as I scribbled JUG EMPTY on my tablet. 'Thanks for the information, Mistress Fotini,' he said. 'The picture is becoming much clearer now. We are one step closer to catching the thief. Goodnight!'

CHAPTER TWELVE

Sour Wine and Rowdy Sailors

I lay on my bed and stared at the jumble of notes in my wax tablet. There was a lot of information there but I couldn't make head nor tail of it. Why had Thrax said we were one step closer to finding the thief?

I desperately wanted to ask him but there were other slaves in the room, checking the amphorae, and by the time they had finished, Thrax was fast asleep.

We did not have time to talk in the morning either. Master Ariston barged into our room before we'd woken up. He was in a foul mood again and even Cook's special breakfast of soft pancakes with honey and milk couldn't put a smile on his face.

'This house is too clean,' he moaned. 'All these polished surfaces are giving me a headache. Nico, fetch your writing implements, we're going to the harbour for inspiration. A glass of sour wine served in a filthy cup will do wonders for my songwriting, I'm sure.'

He turned to Thrax. 'You stay here. I'm going to dye my hair and beard when I get back. Ahmose will show you how to make a special lotion with saffron flowers and potassium water. Make sure you don't use too much potassium water, though, or it will burn my hair off. I don't want to go bald at my tender age.'

'Do you have any spare pine sap?' Thrax asked me while I gathered my writing implements and scrolls.

'Yes, why? Do you want me to make you some ink?'

'No, I need you to make some strong glue. Try not to let anyone see you making it.'

Of course I wanted to find out why Thrax needed a pot of strong glue as well as how we were one step closer to finding the thief. But Master Ariston didn't give me time to ask. He marched me out of the house and down the hill to a seafront tavern. We sat at a rickety table crawling with flies and supped on wine that tasted like vinegar. But the stench of the rubbish tip right next to the tavern and the seagulls squabbling round our feet seemed to meet with Master Ariston's approval.

'This is a place for real people, Nico,' he said, quaffing the sour wine with relish. 'Honest workmen and sailors. The most important citizens in the world and the blessed of the gods.'

There were no important citizens or blessed of the gods about when we started to work, but later in the afternoon several ships docked and soon the harbour was crawling with sailors.

'Which is the quickest way to the temple of Aphrodite, gentlemen?'

'Which way to the Acrocorinth?'

Master Ariston scowled darkly every time we were interrupted. He pointed in the direction of the hill above the town. 'Up there, you couldn't possibly miss it. Hurry up, the priestesses are waiting.'

Before long Master Ariston had had enough interruptions and we returned home. I expected to find Thrax waiting for Master Ariston with the hair dye but he was nowhere to be seen. I went to look for him in the kitchen.

'He said he was going to feed Ariana in the stable,' said Cook, passing me a small almond cake hot off the brazier. 'But the boy's been gone a long time. That donkey must be very hungry.'

I started towards the stable only to see Thrax hurrying back, looking rather smug.

'Have that glue ready for tonight,' he whispered, crossing the yard to Master Ariston's room.

For the next hour or so, the entire household could hear howls of pain coming from my master's window as Thrax applied the dye to his hair and beard.

I used the time to make up the glue that Thrax had asked for, pretending I was mixing a fresh pot of ink. I couldn't for the life of me figure out what he needed it for.

I was soon to find out, though, and our search for the thief was going to take on a whole new dangerous direction.

CHAPTER THIRTEEN

Gold Dust, and a Sinister Face

When Master Ariston finally emerged from his room, I had to try very hard not to laugh. His hair and beard were the colour of a sunflower. Surely Thrax would get into trouble for not mixing the dye right?

But it seemed Master Ariston liked his new coiffure. He admired his reflection in a hand mirror. 'It makes me look years younger,' he sighed. 'I feel... rejuvenated. I am going to perform like Orpheus himself tonight.'

He did indeed perform very well at the symposium. The best I'd ever seen him, if I'm honest. He composed so many songs on the spot, I had difficulty keeping up with him. Not that I was concentrating very hard. My mind kept going back to the pot of glue that I'd hidden behind the amphorae in our room.

'Will you *please* tell me what we're going to use it for?' I begged Thrax when we'd been dismissed for the night.

'Be patient,' he whispered, indicating the door where we'd suspected someone was eavesdropping on us four nights before. 'I'll tell you later. And you're going to need a glue brush. Have you got one?'

'Yes I have, although I don't carry it around with me. I use it to paste sheets of papyrus together to make scrolls.'

I fetched the brush and we lay on our beds, waiting in silence until the only sound we could hear was an owl hooting in the yard. Then we thrust our feet into sandals and tiptoed out of the room. I took the glue with me, and the brush.

Thrax sneaked into the kitchen and returned with a lighted twig from the embers of the cooking fire. We let ourselves out of the back door, closing it gently behind us.

The night was very clear. A bright three-quarter moon shone on the lane that led to the farm. Thrax passed the burning twig to me and leaned over a bush to pull out something hidden behind it. It was a heavy sack, tied securely at the neck. Its contents clinked like silver as he slung it over his shoulder.

We hurried down the lane to the small farm behind the house. The doves cooed dreamily as we passed the newly painted dovecote. Next door in the stables, Ariana whinnied in her sleep.

We reached a barn with shuttered windows and a small mosaic of Dionysus above the door. Thrax let us in, leaving the door open so we could see. There was a faint smell of wine in the barn, as if someone had recently held a party there.

'This place is used for making wine,' said Thrax. 'I discovered it today when I came to feed Ariana. I hid an oil lamp behind one of the vats there. Could you bring it and light it? Then shut the door.'

I found the lamp and soon a warm glow lit the barn. Thrax untied the sack and upended it. Shards of broken pottery cascaded out, forming a pile on the floor.

'These are the remains of Mistress Pandora's wedding vase,' he said. 'I rescued them from the rubbish heap this afternoon after I fed Ariana. We're going to put the vase back together again.'

I threw him a puzzled glance.

'Humour me,' Thrax demanded.

He started sifting through the pieces while I opened the glue pot and put it carefully on the floor. Thrax was silent for a while but at last he picked up a single fragment. 'This was part of the base. It's hollow, look.'

He rubbed his finger inside the shard and held it close to the lamp. His finger glittered with gold dust.

'There *was* something precious in the wedding vase but it was hidden in the hollow base. This is what the thief wanted, not the pot itself. Gaia thought he picked up a piece of broken pottery from the floor but she was wrong. He picked up the golden object hidden in the base, a piece of jewellery perhaps, or a gold nugget. He did the same in the temple of Aphrodite but the short-sighted priestess didn't see him either. He might even have smashed the pots on purpose – the wedding vase because he couldn't climb out of the window with it and the oinoche because he didn't want to be spotted by sailors coming up the hill.'

'How did he know the gold was hidden in the pottery?' I asked.

Thrax looked at the fragments scattered on the floor. 'Let's put the vase back together. It might give us a clue.'

I moved the lamp closer and we started separating the pieces, making different piles for the various parts of the vase: the rest of the base, the round main section, the curved handles and the slender neck shaped like a lily.

It was a laborious and difficult process but at last every piece was sorted. I dipped the brush in my glue pot and we started rebuilding the vase. Despite some missing pieces, a lifelike scene slowly formed in front of our eyes. Here was the picture Gaia had described in such detail. A happy bride going to her new home in a horse-drawn cart. The bridegroom holding the reins in strong, well-shaped hands. And all around, people giving the happy couple a joyful send-off.

'The artist who painted this is very gifted,' said Thrax as we put together the slim neck and the large curved handles. 'I wonder if he signed his work. Not all painters do.'

We inspected the vase closely but could see no signature.

'Perhaps he marked the vase with a little picture,' I said. 'Peleas told us that Scorpius signs his work with a scorpion.'

Thrax said nothing and turned the vase round slowly in the lamplight, peering at it closely. The lamp guttered and I was starting to worry it might run out of oil when he turned to me. 'Eureka!' he said. 'I've found it.'

He traced his fingers over the beautifully drawn figures. 'This picture is full of symbols. The cart is being pulled by horses instead of donkeys, showing us that the bridegroom comes from a wealthy family. He is holding the reins firmly, which means that he will be a strong head of the family. Look, he has a wide chest and very big shoulders to show that he is healthy. The painter has given the bride a chubby face, telling us that she is in good health too. She will have many babies, hopefully boys.'

He turned the vase again so we could see the rest of the picture better. 'Look, there is the goddess Ilithyia, looking down on the couple from the sky. She is blessing the marriage. There are domestic animals behind the cart too: goats and sheep and geese. They are symbols of prosperity. But look at this!'

Thrax rotated the vase one more time. 'Here are friends and neighbours dancing round the wedding cart. They are the sort of people you would expect to see in any district of Athens or Corinth. Young children throwing rose petals, slaves carrying water jugs and farmers coming home with tools over their shoulders.'

He brought the flickering lamp right up to the vase. 'Now look at the back of the dancing crowd? What do you see?'

I peered at the spot Thrax had pointed to. A small figure was hopping merrily from one foot to another, holding one hand above its head. It was hardly visible among the other dancers but there was no denying that scarred face and one glaring eye.

It was a Cyclops.

CHAPTER FOURTEEN

A Gang of Thieves

'How odd,' I said. 'The Cyclops is not usually associated with weddings.'

'You're right,' Thrax agreed. 'When you think of the Cyclops you think of horror and death.'

I inspected the leering face again. 'So why did the painter put him in the scene? Could it be his signature?'

'He wasn't painted by the original artist,' said Thrax. 'Look at him closely. He's not drawn with the same assured hand as the rest of the vase, and his outline is slightly thicker. It was made with a different brush from the other figures.'

I couldn't help admiring Thrax for spotting such a subtle detail. I wouldn't have noticed the difference between the painting styles if I'd stared at the vase the whole day. 'Then who painted him?'

'The Cyclops is a secret mark to identify the vase,' said Thrax. 'It shows we are dealing with more than one criminal, possibly a whole gang. Here's my theory: thieves in Athens steal gold or jewellery from wealthy citizens and take it to a pottery where a gang member works. This man hides the stolen loot in the hollow bases of pots, no doubt without the knowledge of the potter, the painter or the trader, in this case Peleas. He marks the pots with a secret sign that only other gang members will recognise. These are transported to Corinth where a further member of the gang removes the treasure and glues the base back on the pots.'

I stared at the Cyclops. 'But why wasn't the gold simply taken out of the wedding vase in Alcandros's warehouse?'

'Something must have gone wrong with the operation and the vase left the warehouse before that could happen. Then the thief had no choice but to break into Master Zenon's house to get it...'

Without warning we found ourselves in darkness. The lamp had run out of oil.

'We don't need to light it again,' said Thrax. 'Our work here is done.'

I opened the door to let in some moonlight and he put the wedding vase in the sack, slinging it carefully over his shoulder.

'Don't forget your glue and brush,' he warned, checking the floor to make sure we hadn't left any telltale pieces of pottery.

Outside, the doves warbled and we spied Ahmose standing at the dovecote with his back to us. He was holding his hands up to the starry sky as if in prayer, a dove cooing on his left shoulder. Thrax pulled me back into the barn and we watched in silence.

Ahmose called softly and a second dove came fluttering down from the sky. It settled in his

hands and he cupped his fingers gently around it, running his thumbs over its glossy feathers. He whispered something to it, which made it coo softly. Then he placed it in the dovecote.

We waited in the shadows till Ahmose had returned to the house, then hurried in ourselves.

'I wonder what he was up to,' I said as we got ready for bed. 'Looking after doves in the middle of the night! Perhaps he was praying to Aphrodite. Doves are her symbol.'

'Ahmose is Egyptian,' said Thrax, stowing the wedding vase behind the amphorae. 'He prays to Isis not Aphrodite. But it is odd that he wanders around at night. I wonder if it was him listening in on our conversation.'

We got into our beds and I pulled my himation over me. It was chilly in the storeroom.

'Will the traces of gold dust be enough to prove that Gaia is innocent?' I asked. 'It's now obvious that the vase was not smashed by accident. It was broken so that the thief could get at the gold.'

'Unfortunately Gaia can still be seen as the potential thief,' Thrax replied. 'Master Zenon might convince himself that she was bribed by the thieves to retrieve the gold. I know it's dreadful to think that a small child would agree to help criminals, but stranger things have happened. Many a desperate slave has been sent to her death for colluding with criminals. If anything, revealing what we know might put Gaia in bigger danger. We have to continue looking for the thief. Only now we are looking for a whole gang.'

CHAPTER FIFTEEN

A Song of Swallows

The rooster had already crowed by the time I got up the next morning. A delicious smell of pancakes wafted across the yard from the kitchen, making my mouth water. Thrax was coming out of Master Ariston's room with the breakfast dishes as I crossed the yard with my pens and scrolls.

'Master's in a very jovial mood this morning,' he said. 'He wolfed down three large pancakes for breakfast. Try and keep him happy. I need him to agree to something later on.'

Master Ariston clicked his fingers at me when I went in. He was indeed in a happy mood. 'Bring the writing table closer to the window. Apollo has blessed me with some wonderful ideas.'

The guests at that night's symposium were all going to be athletes whose careers Master Zenon sponsored. Master Ariston was very keen to impress them, hoping they would book him for award ceremonies in the future. We worked hard at his new songs all morning and well into the afternoon.

Thrax brought us a late lunch. 'That's a wonderful poem, master, if I may venture a slave's opinion,' he said, putting grapes and olives on the table. 'May I suggest an idea that would make your performance even more sublime?'

Master Ariston reached for the grapes. 'Go ahead, my boy.'

'Why don't you wear a mask while you sing, like actors do on stage? I saw a singer in Attica once and he wore a mask to great effect. The audience loved it.'

'That's a fabulous idea,' cried Master Ariston. 'I could wear a dramatic mask. Or perhaps a comic one. It will give me a certain air of mystery... and hide the wrinkles around my eyes. One mustn't look too old when performing in front of healthy young sportsmen.'

He handed Thrax his purse. 'Go to the agora and buy me two masks, one comic and one tragic. Make sure they're made from linen not cork. Cork brings me out in spots.'

Thrax left to buy the masks and I continued working, wondering what he was up to. It was nearly dark and Ahmose had come round to light the lamps by the time he returned. He was trembling violently and his eyes were red and watery.

Master Ariston gawped at him in horror. 'You foolish boy. I have seen this sickness descend on vain people who venture out in the sun in flimsy clothing. You have sunstroke. Have Cook make you a healing potion with honey and salt and drink it at once. And tell her to rub you down with curdled milk when she has a moment to spare. Stay away from the party tonight. I don't want a trembling weakling beside me when the rest of the andron is going to be filled with healthy young men.'

Thrax slunk off to the kitchen, leaving me to dress Master Ariston myself. The athletes arrived for the party wearing crowns of wild celery. I'd expected them to be haughty and full of self-importance but they behaved more like schoolboys, telling rude jokes and drinking too much wine. They were very taken by Master Ariston's new masks and cheered rowdily every time he took a bow.

During a break in the performance, one of them took me aside.

'I need to relieve myself.'

'There are chamber pots for the guests in the bathroom, sir,' I replied.

'I'm too drunk to use one of those,' giggled the athlete. 'Show me the back door and I'll be all right in the weeds.'

I put down my stylus and scroll. 'This way, sir.'

We crossed the courtyard and I opened the back door to let him out in the lane. He started singing as he leaned against the wall.

'Came, came the swallow
with pleasant seasons
with the beautiful year.
Came, came the swallow
With pleasant twitters
To soothe away my fear.'

I thought his voice was tinged with sadness, as if the song reminded him of something precious he'd lost.

'I like swallows,' said the athlete, smoothing down his chiton when he'd finished. 'They make me think of Rhodes. A beautiful island, Rhodes.' He peered around him. 'Now, where can I wash my hands?'

'There are basins in the bathroom, sir.'

The athlete spoke in a loud whisper. 'Hush, we're being watched. There's someone hiding in that bush over there. I saw it... quiver.'

He curled his hands around his mouth. 'Oi! Come on out, whoever you are. We've seen you.'

A figure in a hooded himation stepped out into the moonlight. It stood frozen for a second, like a statue of Hephaestus surveying his forge, then it threw back its hood. It was Thrax, wearing one of Master Ariston's old himations.

'Hello, young man,' said the athlete. 'Have you been out chasing girls?'

'He's a friend of mine,' I blurted. 'He's suffering from sunstroke.'

The athlete hiccupped. 'The boy looks perfectly healthy to me.'

I had to admit Thrax did seem to have miraculously recovered from his illness.

The athlete noticed his muscles. 'You look as if you could beat me in the ring, young man.' He stuck out his hand. 'My name is Pandion. I am a wrestler.'

Thrax grinned and returned the greeting. 'I've heard of you. You've won crowns at the Isthmian games. Very pleased to meet you.'

'You should start training properly at the gym,' said Pandion, patting Thrax roughly on the back. 'I'll be your trainer and make you a champion like me...' He stopped when he noticed Thrax's shaved head.

'Oh, I'm sorry, young man. I wasn't thinking. I should keep my big mouth shut when I drink. It's so unjust that some people are barred from using the gym or going into politics because they are slaves. We should all be equal in the eyes of the gods.'

He leaned on me and a sad note crept into his voice again. 'The way your friend smiles reminds me of someone from my childhood, someone who was very dear to me and who was cursed by the cruel gods. Let's get back to the party. More wine awaits! Although I mustn't drink myself into complete oblivion. I am going on an important trip to beautiful Rhodes tomorrow. The island of the swallows. Now, sing with me.

'Came, came the swallow...'

We went back into the house and I helped Pandion to his couch. The athletes insisted on playing a rowdy game of kottabos to end the party and it was very late by the time I returned to the storeroom.

Thrax was sitting on the edge of his bed.

'I thank the god Asclepius that you seem recovered,' I said.

Thrax smiled. 'Sunstroke is one of the easiest sicknesses to fake. The juice of a ripe beet to redden the skin and a slice of fresh onion to make the eyes water. The rest is just play-acting.'

'I take it you needed to be out of the house tonight.'

Thrax went to the door to make sure no one was listening. 'I figured if there was one pot with gold in it, there might be more. And the oinoche smashed in the temple could be one of them. Mistress Fotini and I went up to the Acrocorinth during the symposium. We sneaked into the treasury and searched through the broken pieces of the jug.'

'Could you not just have asked the high priestess to let you have them?' I said. 'They can't be worth anything.'

'A smashed vase is still a holy offering to the gods and not the temple's to give away,' replied Thrax. 'The priestesses swept up the pieces and placed them carefully in a little wooden chest, which will be kept forever in the treasure house. They would not have let me touch them if I'd asked.'

Thrax drew a small piece of pottery from under his belt and held it out on the palm of his hand. 'The jug had the mark of the Cyclops too, just like the wedding vase.'

I inspected the piece in the lamplight. A scarred face with only one eye leered back at me. Thrax reached under the bed and pulled out a shiny round object. It was a hollow glass ball with a small hole at the top. He filled it with clear water from the washbasin.

'This is an inspection sphere,' he said. 'The latest in scientific apparatus. Mistress Fotini let me borrow it. Bring the lamp closer.'

He placed the ball carefully on the neck of a small jar on the clothes chest. Then he carefully held the fragment from the pouring jug behind it. Instantly the water in the sphere made the image of the grinning Cyclops look much bigger. It revealed details that we hadn't noticed before.

'Have a look,' Thrax said, 'and tell me what you see.'

I peered through the watery glass. 'The Cyclops is very badly painted,' I said. 'Looks like it was done in a hurry.'

'What else?' asked Thrax.

'He is holding his hand close to his face,' I said. 'I think he is waving.'

'How many fingers on his hand can you count?'

I strained to see through the glass. 'Four, I think. Yes, that's right. He has only four fingers on his hand.'

Thrax put down the piece from the oinoche and replaced it with the one from Mistress Pandora's wedding vase.

'And what can you see now?'

'The Cyclops on this one has four fingers too.'

'I don't think the Cyclops is waving,' said Thrax. 'I think he's holding up four fingers. A sign to the gang that there were four pots coming from Athens. We couldn't see it without the inspection sphere.'

'That means the thieves have an inspection sphere too,' I said, 'or they wouldn't see the mark of the Cyclops clearly.'

'We are dealing with a very well organised gang,' confirmed Thrax, 'and I don't think it's run by uneducated ruffians. There's someone very powerful at the top.'

He put the two pieces of broken pottery carefully in his bag and emptied the glass ball.

'If my theory is right, there are two more Athenian vases that the gang will be after. This is just the lead we need. If we can find out who bought them, we could lay a trap for the gang when they try to steal them.'

'Unless they already have,' I pointed out.

'Chances are that they haven't,' said Thrax. 'I spoke to our friend the stallholder in the agora again yesterday. That part of the market is a hive of gossip but he hadn't heard of any thefts except for the ones in Master Zenon's house and the temple.'

'Alcandros must keep details of all his orders,' I said. 'Is there a way we can look at his books to find out who bought the other two marked pots?'

Thrax placed the inspection sphere in the bag with the pieces of pottery. 'We can't very well ask Donos to show us his master's account books. At least not without raising suspicions. But I have a little plan. Now let's get some sleep. It's almost sunrise.'

CHAPTER SIXTEEN

Spartan Mice

Master Ariston burst into the kitchen in a state of high agitation the next morning. 'I left my favourite himation outside last night,' he wailed. 'I don't know how it happened. I'm always so careful with my clothes. The dew made it shrink. Look, it's too tight around my waist.'

'What a shame,' said Thrax, who was chopping figs for breakfast. 'That himation was old but it fitted you so well.'

Master Ariston looked him up and down. 'You seem much better today. I'm glad the potions I recommended worked so effectively.'

'They worked like magic,' said Thrax with a straight face. 'And don't worry about your himation, master. I've heard of an old seamstress in the agora who can take it out for you at very little cost. It will be much cheaper than buying a new one.'

Master Ariston smiled from ear to ear. 'That's a brilliant idea, Thrax. But make sure she uses good Spartan wool. And make sure you wear my old chlamys when you go out. I don't want you getting ill again. Nico, you go with him and make sure no one takes advantage of him. He was charged double for the masks yesterday.'

Master Ariston settled down to breakfast in a good mood. Thrax was given lots of jobs to do and it was nearly midday before we were free to leave the house.

'It was you who left the himation outside, wasn't it?' I said as we made our way into town. 'You borrowed it to go to the temple of Aphrodite. You knew the dew would make it shrink.'

Thrax laughed cheekily. 'I just wanted to make sure we had the opportunity to continue our investigation today.'

The sun was so hot, a shimmering haze was rising from the dusty road. The streets were deserted except for a lone figure trudging up the hill with a large basket under one arm. Thrax, sweltering in his chlamys, pulled me behind a clump of almond trees.

'Why are we hiding?'

'That man coming up to the house is Donos,' he said. 'I don't want him to see us.'

'Is he visiting Master Zenon?'

'I asked Mistress Fotini to send for him,' said Thrax. 'She's buying some Egyptian perfume bottles. We want to make sure he's safely out of the way for a while.'

We waited until Donos passed the almond trees, cursing in the heat. Then we tore down the street and reached the agora in time to leave the shrunken himation with the old seamstress before she packed up for the afternoon.

When we'd been to the potters' district earlier in the month, the streets had been busy, the workshops ringing with the sound of industry. But now, well past lunchtime, the workshops were shut and all was quiet. The only noise was the shrill song of the cicadas hidden between the stones of the city walls.

We stopped outside Alcandros's warehouse and looked around to make sure no one was watching. Thrax unhooked the pin from his chlamys and deftly picked the lock on the door. Cerberus barked as we stepped into the dark warehouse but Thrax quieted him down with a pat on the head.

'Good boy, Cerberus. So nice to see you again. Down, boy!'

He pulled a large bone out of his bag and thrust it under the dog's nose. Cerberus dragged it behind some shelves, his tail wagging happily.

'Close the door and keep an eye out in case anyone comes,' hissed Thrax. He vaulted over the counter and disappeared into the shadows.

'Here are some scrolls,' he whispered at last. There was the rustle of papyrus as he moved closer to a small window high up in the wall.

'Do you want me to read it for you?' I said.

'I was taught to read by another slave,' replied Thrax. 'And I write too. Although I don't tell many people about it. It's good to have a secret weapon.'

I heard the scratching of pen on papyrus. 'Don't take too long,' I said. 'Cerberus will have finished that bone by now.'

'I think you'll find Cerberus is having an afternoon nap. I dipped the bone in a sleeping potion.'

I heard the scratch of stylus on papyrus as Thrax copied snippets of information from the account books. Then a loud banging at the door made me jump.

'Oi, we know you're in there. Come on out or we'll fetch the law.'

I felt panic rising in my throat. 'Thrax, we've been caught.'

'Leave this to me,' he said, jumping back over the counter. 'Have you got your wax tablet with you?'

'Yes.'

'Open it, and take out your stylus.'

He opened the door and pushed aside the linen curtain. A group of men had gathered on the pavement, most of them plastered from head to toe in dry clay or sawdust.

'Thieves,' one of them shouted. 'We saw you break in.'

Thrax looked around the dishevelled group calmly. 'My colleague and I are scribes from the archon's office. We have a special warrant to search this establishment, signed by the archon himself.' He nodded at me. 'Show them.'

I held out my wax tablet, praying to the gods that none of the men could read. They seemed to swallow the bait.

'The office of the archon has been informed that there is an infestation of poisonous mice from Sparta in this establishment. They must have been brought to our fair city unknowingly, hidden in imported merchandise. I can't tell you how dangerous and destructive Spartan mice are. Their sharp teeth gnaw through wood and baked clay. If they were to invade our city, the very foundations of Corinth would crumble within a month.'

He glared round at the men. 'Thanks be to Demeter we found no Spartan mice in Alcandros's shop today. Perhaps our trusted informant was wrong. However, they might be hiding in one of your establishments.'

The men looked at each other in alarm and Thrax turned to me. 'Please take these men's names so we can search their workshops. I'm sure they won't mind, being the honest citizens they are.'

The men started muttering among themselves and a few backed away from the group. These were poor citizens who could only survive by bending a few rules here and there. None of them were keen to be seen colluding with the law.

'I sense an unfortunate reluctance to co-operate with us,' said Thrax severely. 'Very well. My colleague and I will let the matter pass for today. But if we have one more report about Spartan mice invading the potters' district, we'll have to investigate further.'

He locked the door to Alcandros's shop with the pin from his chlamys, so deftly that no one in the crowd noticed the trick. 'Come on,' he said to me, 'we have one more establishment in the silversmiths' district to inspect this afternoon. An infestation of Thracian snakes, I believe.'

I stuck my wax tablet under one arm and the group parted meekly to let us through. 'Good day, gentlemen,' said Thrax brazenly. 'May the divine Hera smile upon you all.'

We marched smartly up the road leaving the men dumbfounded. Once safely past the ruined temple, I breathed a sigh of relief.

'Do you think they believed us?' I said on our way back to the agora to fetch the altered himation.

'It doesn't matter if they did or not,' laughed Thrax. 'We cooked up such a preposterous story no one will believe *them* if they talk. There's no such thing as a Spartan mouse. Donos will come back to find the door to the warehouse properly locked, nothing missing or out of place and Cerberus wide awake again.'

'Here he comes now,' I said as we trudged up the hill to Master Zenon's house.

Thrax pulled me behind the clump of almond trees again and we waited until the potter was gone. 'Peleas brought ninety-five pieces of pottery from Athens,' he said as we resumed our way home. 'But only six of them are the kind that would have a base large enough to hide something inside. I made a note of them.'

He showed me the scrap of papyrus.

1 loutrophoros decorated with wedding scene (for Sosicles the runner)

1 krater, large, showing Zeus with thunderbolts (for Pernicius the oracle)

1 krater, small, showing Pan dancing with goats (also for Pernicius the oracle)

1 oinoche decorated with Aphrodite swimming (for the chief priestess of Aphrodite)

1 lekythos, decorated with sportsmen and swallows (for Polydeuces of Rhodes)

1 hydria, decorated with dancers and satyrs (for Euripides the playwright)

'Only four of these would have the mark of the Cyclops. The smashed loutrophoros, the oinoche and another two.'

'I wonder which two.'

'That,' said Thrax, 'is what we have to find out next.'

CHAPTER SEVENTEEN

Trouble at the Theatre

We had no more time to discuss the case because we had now reached Master Zenon's house and we had to prepare for that night's symposium. The guests that evening were all famous merchants and politicians. Master Zenon was currying favour with the great and good of Corinth. Perhaps he had ambitions to become an archon himself.

Halfway through the party, Thrax sneezed very loudly. Master Ariston nearly jumped off his three-legged stool and clutched the lyre to his chest.

Thrax's face was once more an alarming red. This time I knew it was a trick but I had no idea how he'd made himself up right there in the andron without anyone noticing. The boy was a genius.

'You have the sun sickness again,' Master Ariston hissed angrily. 'Make yourself a soothing medicine and go to bed. I hope you'll be better by tomorrow morning. I have tickets for the first performance of *Alcestis* in Corinth and I won't be seen at the theatre without my personal slave.'

Thrax left the room trying to look shamefaced and I didn't see him again till the early hours of the morning.

'Where have you been? The rooster is about to crow. Cook is already making breakfast.'

'I called on Euripides the playwright, hoping to see the hydria he bought from Alcandros. I didn't tell him I'd gone to see the pot, of course. I pretended I needed some fatherly advice about a girl. Remember, he said we could go and see him if we needed help with anything in Corinth. Euripides loves helping slaves.'

We continued talking as we started getting ready for the theatre. 'And did you get a look at the vase?'

'No. Euripides gave it to Mikon the actor as a present. He's using it in the play. Which is very lucky for us. The thief or some other member of the gang has ransacked Euripides's rooms twice, looking for the pot. By now their spies in the city will have found out that Mikon has it. They might try to steal it from the theatre this morning. And if they do, I shall be lying in wait to catch them.'

The road was shiny with morning dew as we made our way to town, Master Ariston hugging a tasselled cushion to sit on in the theatre. A sea fret was drifting in from the harbour, casting a thin veil over the streets. It made the people around us look like shades from the underworld.

Despite the early hour, people were already coming out of the theatre from another play. Master Ariston pushed his way through the crowds, determined to get a seat in the front row.

'I'll stay at the back with the other slaves,' said Thrax as we passed through the gate. 'Signal to me if you need anything.'

'You forget about me and watch the play,' replied Master Ariston grandly, forgetting the fuss he'd made about being seen at the theatre without his slave. 'A spot of culture will do you good. Nico and I will be fine.'

He spotted someone in a flat-brimmed hat waddling down the aisle. 'Oh look, it's Odius the archon. What luck! Let's go and sit with him.'

We caught up with the magistrate who was also trying to find a seat in the front row. He had an extremely old slave with him, who carried a large pile of brightly-embroidered pillows.

'Good morning, sir,' called Master Ariston.

The archon smiled and his bushy eyebrows rose up his forehead like fluffy clouds. 'If it isn't the poet from the *Danais*. Aristus, isn't it?'

'Ariston.'

'Of course it is. I'm not very good with names, I'm afraid. How are the gods treating you?

'They treat me very generously indeed, may their names be praised. Would you mind if we sat with you?'

'But of course,' said the archon, finding an empty seat and inspecting it for dust. His slave gave it a quick wipe with a cloth and placed the cushions on it. 'Have you brought your muscled young slave with you?'

'He's at the back with the other slaves,' said Master Ariston.

The archon's impressive eyebrows knitted together. 'My slave is going to sit at my feet right here at the front. He enjoys a well-written play. I don't hold with this nonsense of keeping slaves at the back of the theatre. Some of them have finer minds than all these free citizens hogging the front rows.'

'Quite,' agreed Master Ariston, sounding rather taken aback by the archon's comment.

I looked around me. The theatre was full to bursting and there was a hum of excitement as the audience waited for the play to start. The sound of musicians tuning up wafted out from behind the stage. Then a priest appeared onstage and offered a sacrifice to Dionysus at a small altar, pouring wine on to it from a rhyton shaped like a bull's head. By now the sun had fully risen, filling the theatre with golden light. The sound of an aulos floated across the stage and an actor dressed as Dionysus skipped out of the wings. I leaned forward in my seat, putting all thoughts of Thrax and smashed vases out of my mind. The play had begun.

It was a powerful story. Queen Alcestis, played by the much-admired Mikon in a female mask, died in the arms of her husband. Tanatos, the lord of death, dragged her away to the underworld, to spend the rest of eternity as a shade.

Her husband, King Admetus was so racked with grief, he swore never to play music again. But then along came his best friend Herakles, victorious from a battle and wanting to celebrate. He demanded food, wine... and music. And King Admetus, not wanting to offend his best friend, entertained him with his lyre, breaking his promise to his dead wife.

When Herakles discovered his mistake he travelled to the underworld and rescued Queen Alcestis, bringing her back to the palace. King Admetus begged her forgiveness but the queen, standing still in her mask, did not reply.

'She is still under Tanatos's deathly spell,' declared Herakles. 'And she will remain so until she has washed the dust of the underworld from her hair.'

King Admetus called for his slaves. 'Bathe her with water from a sacred spring that she might speak to me again. Anoint her with unguents and perfumes...'

Suddenly the stage was filled with members of the chorus bearing jars of ointment and lotions. One of them held a beautiful water jug decorated with glowing red figures in the style of Athenian pottery.

I sat forward in my seat. This was Mikon's hydria, the present from Euripides. The actor tipped it slowly and mimed pouring water over Mikon in the queen's mask. Mikon trembled dramatically to show that Tanatos's deadly spell was broken.

'I love you, my husband. My children, I swear to look after you and protect you for the rest of my life.'

'Blessed be Herakles, and blessed be the gods,' said the actor playing King Admetus. He took the hydria and raised it above his head. 'This jug has washed away the curse of Tanatos and the gods decree that it shall never be used by a mortal again. I shall break it to pieces on the floor...'

There was a scream from the chorus as a masked figure leaped out of the wings and landed right behind King Admetus. It was a tall, thick-set man with scars all the way up his right arm and a hideous one-eyed mask.

The Cyclops!

He snatched the hydria out of the startled actor's hands and, surprisingly nimble for his size, leaped off the stage again. He landed on his feet in front of the archon, who gasped loudly. Then he raced up the aisle and vanished through one of the exits.

There was confusion onstage as the actors tried to work out who had invaded the theatre.

The man playing Dionysus was hastily lowered down in a wooden crane. 'Thus the gods say the story endeth,' he announced shakily. 'And thus finishes our humble play.'

The audience roared its approval. No one had guessed that the daring theft was a real crime and not part of the performance, not even Master Ariston and the archon.

'Euripides is such a clever playwright,' we overheard a young priest say loudly as we made our way towards the exit. 'That last scene was pure satire. It poked fun at all the rumours going round Corinth that a thief is stealing precious pots from the houses of the rich. What genius!'

'I don't think this new version of *Alcestis* is a work of genius at all,' declared Master Ariston in an embarrassingly loud voice. 'By the power of Apollo, I could have written a much more fitting ending to such a romantic story.'

Thrax was waiting outside the theatre when we came out. I could tell by the frown on his face that he was disappointed with himself.

He'd come so close to the thief but somehow his plan had gone wrong.

That was the last we'd see of the third marked pot. Now we only had one chance left to catch the Cyclops red-handed and bring him to justice.

CHAPTER EIGHTEEN

The Last Vase

Master Ariston came home from the theatre convinced he could be a successful playwright. He kept me working through the morning on a playscript, a love story about Zeus and Hera. I did not have the chance to talk to Thrax till late in the afternoon.

'I was expecting the thief to steal the pot after the play when all the props were packed away,' he explained. 'But he must have been waiting in the wings. And when he heard King Admetus announce that he was going to smash the hydria, he must have thought it was going to happen for real. So he dived onstage and made off with it. I have to say that daring escape through the audience was inspired.'

'You weren't to know any of that was going to happen,' I comforted him, looking at the list of vases on the scrap of papyrus.

We crossed out the items that had already been stolen.

~~1 loutrophoros decorated with wedding scene (for Sosicles the runner)~~
1 krater, large, showing Zeus with thunderbolts (for Pernicius the oracle)
1 krater, small, showing Pan dancing with goats (also for Pernicius the oracle)
~~1 oinoche decorated with Aphrodite swimming (for the chief priestess of Aphrodite)~~
1 lekythos, decorated with sportsmen and swallows (for Polydeuces of Rhodes, to be collected)
~~1 hydria, decorated with actors, dancers and satyrs (for Euripides the playwright)~~.

'I wonder which one of these remaining pots is the marked one?' I said.

'It's the lekythos,' said Thrax, crossing out the kraters. 'Pernicius the oracle holds fortune-telling meetings in his andron. I slipped out and attended one of them while you and Master Ariston were writing yesterday. The kraters were on display in his meeting room. They are not marked.'

'That does only leave the lekythos,' I said, 'bought by someone called Polydeuces of Rhodes.'

'I asked after Polydeuces at the agora,' said Thrax. 'No one's heard of him. It must be a false name.'

'That must be why the fourth pot hasn't been found yet,' I said. 'The thieves are looking for someone who doesn't exist.'

Thrax held out the papyrus. 'It says here that the lekythos is decorated with athletes and swallows. Who does that remind you of?'

'Pandion the wrestler at the party. He sang about swallows and said they reminded him of Rhodes. Polydeuces claims he comes from Rhodes, and Pandion said he was going to Rhodes. That's a connection if I ever saw one. Do you think it was Pandion the wrestler who ordered the lekythos?'

'Yes.'

'But why would he order it under a false name?'

'Who do you associate Polydeuces with?'

'Polydeuces is a famous character in mythology. He's a demi-god whose brother Castor died because he was a mortal. Polydueces agreed to share his immortality with him and Zeus turned both them into the twin stars so that they could be together forever in the heavens. Do you think Pandion has a twin like Polydeuces and he used the name as a tribute?'

Thrax nodded. 'I think he *had* a twin but he died when they were young. Do you remember he told you my smile reminded him of someone from his childhood, someone very dear to him? He must have been talking about a twin brother. A secret brother. My guess is that Pandion and his brother were born in Rhodes as slaves. Then a rich couple adopted Pandion and brought him up in Corinth as their own flesh and blood. They didn't adopt his brother because he had some kind of physical defect. Perhaps he was lame or blind. Remember, Pandion said he was cursed by the gods.

'I spoke to Euripides about him yesterday. His parents are great patrons of the arts and the playwright has met them at social gatherings. There's gossip about them. No one knows where they're really from. They popped up in Corinth when Pandion was already old enough to train at the gym.'

'But why hide the fact that Pandion is adopted?' I asked.

'There is shame for couples who cannot have children,' said Thrax. 'Foolish people believe they are cursed. The same people think children without perfect bodies are punishments from the gods. They must have made Pandion promise he would never reveal the truth about his lowly birth or his imperfect brother. So when he ordered a new lekythos for his brother's grave, he told his slave to give a false name.'

'Pandion must have gone to Rhodes to visit the grave.'

'And to mark it with a new lekythos.'

'That means we can never hope to catch the thief trying to steal it.'

Thrax put away the scrap of papyrus. 'Pandion's lekythos has given me an idea. We can still try to trap the Cyclops, but we have to do it tonight. The wedding is tomorrow and we'll be leaving Corinth after that.'

My heart sank as I realised what he meant. We only had one day left to save Gaia.

CHAPTER NINETEEN

Shadows in the Graveyard

The sun was already low in the sky as Thrax and I slipped out of the back door. The house was humming with activity. Women were arriving for the last of Mistress Pandora's ceremonies. They were dressed in flowing robes and carried flasks of wine or baskets of ripe fruit. Some of them were drunk.

High up in the Acrocorinth, the priestesses of Aphrodite were burning sacrifice at the door of the temple. The smoke from their altar rose up into the fading sky like a dark column. Below us, the agora lay under a thin veil of evening mist. It made me think of a dead man on a pallet, waiting to be carried to his funeral.

It was getting chilly and I was glad I had put on my himation and boots. Thrax didn't seem to mind the cold. He was wearing a tattered himation but only sandals on his feet. A large bag was slung over his shoulder, bumping against his back as he walked. I carried a parcel too, hidden under my own himation. It was an old water jug Thrax had borrowed from the storeroom.

'Remember, I am going to pretend to be Polydeuces of Rhodes and you are my slave,' he said. 'We are going to offer sacrifice at the tomb of my parents, Cylon and Adelpha, and we're using a lekythos in honour of my dead brother Leonidas who is buried with them.'

I tightened my grip on the water jug under my cloak. It was getting heavier as I walked. 'Cylon and Adelpha? Is there really such a grave?'

'Yes,' said Thrax. 'I found it earlier today while you were working. I also stopped at the agora and announced that my master, Polydeuces of Rhodes, was offering sacrifice at his brother's grave tonight. You can be sure that the thief's spies have told him the news by now. Then I paid a quick visit to the archon. He's sending some of his men to help us. They'll be lying in wait close to the tomb.'

The sun had almost set as we neared the city gates. A guard was lighting a fire in a copper brazier and he waved us through without even looking up.

'Draw your himation over your head,' said Thrax. 'We don't want to be recognised.'

We both covered our heads as the city gates swung shut behind us. Ahead lay a wide road with a long line of ancient cypress trees on either side. It made me shudder just to look at them. Cypress trees are symbols of death. Legend has it that if you sleep in their shade, their roots will sap your brain, turning you into one of the undead.

Above us the darkening sky was full of twittering swallows and somewhere an early owl hooted. Huddled together between the tree trunks we could see dozens of tombstones. They stood in jagged lines, some of them leaning at odd angles like the waxy teeth of old men.

Behind the cypress trees, the ground rose steeply, forming two grassy hills. They were both covered in more graves, some marked with just a funerary vase, others with elaborately carved tombstones.

'We are walking in the valley of death,' I whispered to Thrax.

'And we are being followed already,' he whispered back. 'I just caught a glimpse of a shadow darting behind the tombstones to my right.'

I started to turn but Thrax grabbed my arm. 'Don't look round. We mustn't let them know we're expecting anyone. Just walk at a normal pace.'

We continued in silence and soon we came to a tall umbrella pine, its twisted branches reaching out across the road.

'We turn right here,' said Thrax and we left the paved road and started up the hill. The graves here were more widely spaced and a few had lamps burning on them. Some of the tombstones were ancient. The stone carvings on them had worn away or were covered in lichen.

It was dark now. We passed a couple offering sacrifice at a small tomb. They had a fire burning, which lit up the gravestone. I noticed the carving on the headstone: a small boy holding a dog on a leash. He must have been their son.

Thrax took an unlit torch from under his cloak and gestured at them, asking if he might light it at their fire.

The man nodded. 'Go ahead.'

Now that we had a light, we could see more clearly. The shadow that had followed us on the road was still with us. I noticed it darting between two tombstones, its himation flapping like a bat. But was it a thief or one of the archon's men, waiting to help us?

'Look,' said Thrax. 'Here's the tomb.'

Cylon and Adelpha's grave was very elaborate, a rectangular stone shaped like an altar. The carving showed two people seated at a table. The man was holding a dove and the woman a pomegranate, an offering to Persephone, queen of the underworld. They stared back at me with empty eyes. Below the carving, their names were written in stone, in the hope that people would remember them. A third name, Leonidas, showed that their son was buried here too.

Thrax stood the burning torch in the soil so that it threw flickering shadows all around us. It made the graveyard look like the entrance to Hades itself.

I guarded the water jug while Thrax cleared the tomb of debris. My heart was pounding in my chest. This was the closest I had come to physical danger since the ambush on the Isthmus.

Thrax spread the contents of his bag on the tomb: fruit, vegetables and a small loaf of bread. Then he scooped up armfuls of dry weeds, piling them high to cover the offerings.

Thrax held the torch to the weeds and the altar lit up with roaring flames. 'Oh my father, Cylon,' he called out, 'my mother, Adelpha, and my

brother, Leonidas, we come tonight to pronounce your name that it might live long in our memory. And to honour Leonidas with wine from a new lekythos.'

He gestured at me and I unwrapped the bundle to reveal the water jug. Thrax took it, pulled out the stopper and poured wine on the altar.

The fire hissed, the dying flames plunging the graveyard back into near-darkness. I heard a loud grunt behind me, then a hooded figure leaped towards us. Two more figures joined it, knocking me out of the way as they tried to wrestle the water jug from Thrax.

I looked around for the archon's men but there was no movement in the darkness. 'Help,' I cried. 'We're under attack!'

But we seemed to be alone with the thieves. We had been forgotten or the gang had bribed the archon's men to stay away.

One of our assailants kicked Thrax in the stomach, sending him reeling to the ground. He snatched the water jug from his arms. 'Got it, men. Let's go.'

'Wait!' Thrax got to his knees, gasping for air. 'That's not the lekythos you're looking for. It's just an old water jug.'

The men stopped dead in their tracks and turned in unison towards us. The one holding the water jug was standing very close to Thrax's torch and the flames lit his face under the hood.

His eyes were bright with fury.

CHAPTER TWENTY

Prisoners

One of the other men yanked the torch out of the ground and held it over the water jug.

'It's true. This is a worthless piece of rubbish.'

His accomplice hurled the jug across the graveyard and it shattered against a headstone. The third man hissed, 'Where's our lekythos?'

'We don't have it.'

The men looked at each other under their hoods and one of them nodded an agreement. 'Take them to the captain.'

The other two dived at us and I was dragged to the ground by strong muscular hands. There was the sound of tearing cloth as one of the men tore strips off his himation to make blindfolds. I was bound and gagged, the strips of cloth biting so deep into my wrists that my hands went instantly numb.

One of our captors pulled me back to my feet and I was dragged roughly down the hill, my boots slipping on the wet grass. Thrax was close behind me, grunting angrily through his gag.

After a while the grass was replaced by hard ground. We had come to the ancient umbrella pine by the road. The thieves bundled me on to a cart and Thrax was thrust in after me. The wooden boards creaked as one of the men clambered on board with us, pushing me roughly aside to make room for his bulk. I could smell damp clay on his tunic.

The Cyclops.

He leaned towards me and I felt the tip of a knife prick my chest. 'One false move from either of you and you'll be back in the graveyard for good.'

The cart started moving, the donkey's hooves clip-clopping on the paving stones. I wondered which direction we were going. Back towards Corinth, or the other way, to the harbour in Cenchreae?

Before long we stopped and the driver spoke to someone in hushed, urgent tones. There was the clink of money exchanging hands. I heard the rasp of a wooden bolt being drawn across wood, followed by the light creak of well-oiled metal hinges. The thieves had bribed a guard to open the city gate. We were back in Corinth.

We trundled through and I heard the gate close again. I hoped the noise would bring someone to a window, but if it did no one spoke or called. Soon the cart turned a corner and a metal door crashed shut behind it.

The Cyclops pulled me roughly off the cart. Another door opened and I stumbled over a doorstep. My feet were kicked from under me, making me fall backwards into a seat. The gag was removed from my mouth.

I heard water burbling faintly, and birds tweeting, then the clink of a beaded curtain being parted.

'Captain,' said one of our captors, 'we went to the graveyard as instructed but we did not get the lekythos. Master Polydeuces here tricked us.'

'I am not Polydeuces of Rhodes,' said Thrax in a seat next to me. 'I am an impostor. My friend and I played a trick on your henchmen, Captain.' The seat creaked as he leaned forward. 'You might have bought off the archon's men but I took the precaution of having a backup plan. There was an unseen witness to your men's attack on us tonight. And that witness has summoned the law. It should be at the door any moment.'

This was the first time I'd heard of a backup plan. Had Thrax really hired a witness to shadow us? Who would that be? There was only one person that I knew Thrax would trust. Mistress Fotini. She must have been the hooded figure I saw following us.

A loud banging made me jump in my seat. 'Open this door in the name of the law.'

It was a voice I recognised at once. Odius the archon himself had come to our rescue.

CHAPTER TWENTY ONE

Thrax Explains the Mystery

I heard the archon's laboured breathing as he stomped into the room. 'Remove their blindfolds immediately. And untie their hands. These boys are personal friends of mine.'

The ties and blindfold were taken off at once and I saw that we were in a large comfortable room. It was decorated in an exotic style with coloured-glass lamps, caged birds and an indoor fountain. The captain was sitting behind a large table. He had a narrow face, with prominent cheekbones and long black hair swept back from his forehead. His eyes were very dark, the colour of mature olives. I turned to see who else was in the room but the hooded thieves had slipped out, leaving Thrax and me with only the archon and the captain.

Mikon's hydria stood on the table in front of him.

'I see your thugs have not smashed it yet,' said Thrax.

'We are not in the habit of destroying works of art if we can help it,' replied the captain. 'But sometimes we have no choice.'

'Thrax,' said the archon. 'Would you like to tell me why I am here?'

'We have unmasked a gang of smugglers and thieves, your honour,' said Thrax.

The archon's extraordinary eyebrows quivered like rainclouds about to release a heavy downpour. 'Have you indeed? Tell me everything you know.'

He settled on a pillowed couch and Thrax started his explanation of the case. 'As you

might have heard, your honour, just a few days ago the loutrophoros that Master Sosicles bought Mistress Pandora for their wedding was smashed. A young slave was blamed for the accident and Master Zenon now wants to sell her. His daughter, Mistress Fotini, hired me to find the real culprit, a thief wearing a Cyclops mask.

'Four days later there was a similar theft, this time an oinoche from the temple of Aphrodite. It too was smashed on the scene of the crime, leading me to think that the thefts were connected.

'I inspected the remains of both the wedding vase and the pouring jug and in both I found a detail that not had been drawn by the original vase painter. It was the face of a Cyclops, a mark that was for only someone who knew it existed.

'I also found traces of gold dust inside the hollow base of the wedding vase, and from this I concluded that gold was being smuggled from Athens to Corinth in the bases of the pots, which were marked for identification.

'All this was done by a gang of smugglers without the knowledge of the honest vase makers and their agents. Someone working for the gang travelled with the pots from Athens to make sure they didn't get lost among piles of similar wares, and to tell the gang members in Corinth what the secret mark was.

'Only on a recent journey, where you yourself were present, something went wrong with the plan. Tanoutamon was not only one of Peleas's slaves, he was also a member of the gang. So when he was killed in a bandit raid on the Diolkos, he could no longer identify the mark to the gang members in Corinth. By the time they got word of the sign from Athens, the marked pots had been delivered to the people who'd ordered them, and the gang had to try and steal them back, or at least the gold hidden inside them.

'Nico and I worked out there were two more marked pots beside the loutrophoros and the oinoche. We thought we could use one of them to lead us to the thief. But when the third one slipped through our fingers, and with the fourth already out of the city, we had to use a fake.'

The archon looked at him with wide, soulful eyes. 'A fantastic story, my boy, and one that should be written for young people to read, but do you have any proof of all this?'

Thrax nodded at the hydria on the captain's table. 'If I'm right, there should be gold in the base of that pot.' He turned to me. 'Nico, can I borrow your sharpening knife, please?'

I gave him the knife from my bag. Thrax turned the hydria over and stood it on its head. Slowly, he ran the tip of my knife along the groove between the thick base and the belly of the jug. Then he thrust the knife into it and wiggled it. The base and the belly of the hydria parted with a loud pop and something tumbled out on to the table.

But it wasn't the gold we were expecting.

It was just a rolled-up piece of cheap papyrus!

CHAPTER TWENTY TWO

The Gang Revealed

The archon picked it up and slowly unrolled it, his eyebrows rising higher up his brow as he realised what the contents were. 'Why, this is better than gold, Captain. We have been donated a treasure map.'

The captain threw the archon a worried look. 'Your honour...'

'Oh hush, Captain,' said the archon. 'These young men have discovered our secret. I shall not go on pretending they have been imagining things. I know them to be just and intelligent. We could do with brains like theirs in our organisation. I think they should know who we really are.'

The captain looked from Thrax to me. 'If you listen to this, you will be bound to keep it a secret forever. On pain of death!'

'Sit, sit,' said the archon, flapping his chubby hands till Thrax and I returned to our seats. He bowed at Thrax. 'I have to congratulate you, young man. You have solved a mystery I thought no one would. You have a brilliant and enquiring mind. That is why I am going to reveal a deep secret about myself. I am a respected archon but I am also a member of a secret society, a gang if you like. Just like the captain here, who is a high-ranking official in the Corinthian navy. But we do not break the law. At least we didn't until this unfortunate episode with the missing pots forced us to carry out a few break-ins. And, the gods willing, we will never have to again.

'But what is this gang, I hear you ask? Why does it smuggle gold from one city-state to another?'

The captain took over from the archon. 'Have you ever heard of the Eranoi?'

'It's a financial institution,' said Thrax. 'It lends money to people who need to pay off their debts.'

'It also lends money to slaves who want to buy their freedom,' explained the captain. 'But if they don't repay the loan on time, the Eranoi sells them back into slavery to recoup its money. And that's where we come in. Our secret society lends money to freed slaves in danger of being sold back. We're often their last hope. We do not charge our clients interest. Instead we rely on rich gifts donated by wealthy citizens sympathetic to the cause. Many of them, like the archon and myself, are freed slaves themselves who have made good. Others are just kind people who detest slavery.'

He held up the map. 'When we find this treasure, it will help free many others.'

'But why go to the trouble of smuggling gold from one city-state to another?' asked Thrax. 'It's not a crime to help others less fortunate than yourself.'

'We live in a world built on slavery,' said the captain. 'If all slaves were free, our civilization would collapse. Or so the rich believe. It's the reason why our donors insist on keeping their charitable work a secret. They can't be seen to oppose slavery or they would make powerful enemies.'

'Our society has no name,' said the archon. 'It makes it easier to keep its existence a secret. You are both exceptional young men and we hope that one day when you are needed, you will join us... Do we hope in vain?'

Thrax was silent for a brief moment. 'You do not, sir.'

'You do not,' I echoed.

'Excellent,' said the archon. 'We shall drink to seal the agreement.'

'There is one piece of the puzzle that I have not yet worked out,' said Thrax as the captain filled the wine cups. 'How did your people in Athens send information about the mark to their friends in Corinth so quickly?'

'They used doves as message carriers. The man in charge of them in Corinth is Ahmose, Zenon the Younger's chief-of-staff. He too is a member of our secret society.'

'And why was the secret mark a Cyclops?'

The archon shrugged. 'There's no real meaning behind it. Our men in Athens use a different mark every time they send gold to Corinth. It makes it more difficult to spot should anyone infiltrate our organisation. This time it was a Cyclops.'

'So it was just a coincidence that the thief chose to wear a Cyclops mask?'

In answer, the archon called out. 'Bek!'

The bead curtain parted and the now familiar hooded figure of the thief strode into the room. 'Bek,' said the archon. 'Show them your face.'

The thief threw back his hood and I had to stop myself from gasping. The man had a livid scar running down one side of his face. And he only had one eye. He really was a Cyclops!

'That was the only mistake you made, Thrax,' chuckled the archon. 'Bek was not wearing a mask when he climbed into Pandora's room. His previous master plucked out his eye as punishment for staring at him while he ate. The slave girl saw his real face.

'Bek used to be a talented vase painter himself before the horrific punishment robbed him of one eye and his livelihood. You see, the poor man never got over the shock and his hands tremble all the time. You wouldn't notice unless you knew it but it means he can't handle a brush any more. He works as a potter's assistant in a small establishment that makes chamber pots now. When he's not helping out with the cause, of course. That always comes first. Poor Bek. He was devastated when he accidentally dropped the vase – twice! He can't bear destroying beautiful works of art. Usually the pots are opened in front of witnesses who take note of the valuables inside. The captain was waiting for me to open the hydria.'

He stood up and raised his cup. 'I'm glad we have spoken, boys. You may not hear from me for a long time but, one day, when the need arises, I shall send for you. Remember, you have given your word. Bek can take you home now. It's nearly sunrise and I believe you have a wedding to attend.'

CHAPTER TWENTY THREE

The Wedding Feast

It was light by the time Ahmose unlocked the front door to let us in. Thrax's suspicions about him had been right. It must have been Ahmose trying to eavesdrop on our secret conversations. But we were on the same side now. The side of freedom and justice.

Mistress Pandora and her bridesmaids had already left the house and gone to the temple of Aphrodite. They returned not much later than us, Mistress Pandora carrying a new loutrophoros from Athens. She had filled it with water from the sacred spring and would it use for her bridal bath.

The women filed upstairs and soon we could hear the sound of chanting and the splash of water. The slaves set up two tables in the yard, decorating them with coloured tablecloths and flowers.

It was late afternoon by the time Mistress Pandora was ready for her wedding feast. By now all the guests had arrived, fanning themselves to keep cool. Even though Ahmose had set up the awning, the heat was stifling.

Thrax and I sat on either side of Master Ariston as he plucked at his lyre and performed his songs. They were sung only in honour of the bride and her family. The groom would not be at this celebration, which was the last meal the bride would have in her father's house. He would come and fetch her later in the wedding cart, to take her to her new home.

At last there was a loud cheer in the women's quarters and Mistress Fotini appeared at the top of the stairs wearing a blue flowing robe. 'Please be upstanding for the bride.'

Mistress Pandora appeared behind her and came regally down the stairs in a white veil, holding a bunch of wild narcissi. Her mother, relatives and slaves followed, scattering rice and flower petals in her path.

To my surprise, Gaia was with them. Fotini must have fetched her from the temple, hoping her father would not dare carry out his foul threat on his daughter's wedding day. I felt sorry for the girl. She looked ill at ease and kept throwing sidelong glances at Master Zenon while holding tightly to Mistress Fotini's hand.

'It's a pity that we have unmasked the thief but cannot save Gaia,' I said to Thrax behind Master Ariston's back.

'The gods work in mysterious ways,' he replied, giving me a cheeky wink.

I wanted to ask what that comment meant but just then the bride took her seat and Master Ariston launched into another song. The wedding celebration had begun. Ahmose, dressed for the occasion in lavish Egyptian clothes, approached the men's table. He was holding a kantharos with two enormous handles.

'Master, I have served you for many years and I thank the gods of my country – Horus and Isis – for sending me to such a kind master. Please accept this token of my gratitude on such a joyous day.'

He placed the drinking cup in front of Master Zenon whose face lit up with delight. 'Thank you, Ahmose. I too am blessed to have you in my life. You have been a loyal slave for many years. You have provided me with a serene home and protected my family while I travelled abroad. In honour of this great day, I release you from bondage. You are from this moment on a free man although I hope you will stay on in my house as a paid chief-of-staff.'

A gasp went round the yard as people realised the importance of the occasion. 'Thank you, master,' said Ahmose. 'May the gods grant us both a long life and may Hecate give you as many grandchildren as there are seeds in a fig.' He nodded at a slave who came forward with an amphora and filled Master Zenon's new drinking cup. 'I propose a toast. To Master Zenon.'

Everyone in the yard held up their dinking cup, including the children. 'To Master Zenon.'

Master Zenon raised his cup but his smile turned into a puzzled frown as a shadow fell across the yard. There was a loud, angry roar and something came hurtling down from the roof, taking the awning with it.

The guests panicked and there was confusion as the slaves tried to free them from under layers of flapping cloth. Then Gaia let out a piercing scream. 'IT'S THE CYCLOPS!'

And there, standing in the remnants of the awning, was Bek, his one good eye fixed on Master Zenon's new drinking cup. He leaped at it and deftly plucked it out of his hands. A moment later, he had run up the stairs to the women's quarters, blood-red wine spilling on to the stairs. Ahmose chased him into the gynaikeion and we heard the sound of a scuffle before he returned with the empty cup, holding it high above his head like a trophy.

'I am sorry the thief managed to escape, sir,' he said to Master Zenon over the cheering of the guests. 'But blessed be the gods I managed to rescue the cup.'

Master Zenon gawped at him like a landed fish. Then he turned to Gaia. 'I apologise profusely for calling you a liar, little one,' he grunted. 'Forget the threats of a foolish man. There really is such a thing as a Cyclops.'

CHAPTER TWENTY FOUR

The Medusa League

'That was quite an impressive drama you thought up,' laughed Mistress Fotini when Thrax and I went to see her later. 'I must congratulate Ahmose on his acting skills too. It was very convincing.'

The wedding was over. Mistress Pandora had gone to live in her husband's house, taking her personal slave and a good dowry with her. Thrax and I were about to return to Athens. We had already said goodbye to Ahmose, Euripides and our new friend Bek. Now it was time to say goodbye to Mistress Fotini and Gaia too.

Mistress Fotini smiled happily. 'Thank you for saving Gaia.' She nodded at her slave who opened a chest to draw out a purse.

'I thank you too,' Gaia said shyly. 'I am glad you believed me when I said that a Cyclops had smashed the wedding vase.'

Thrax took the purse, squeezing it under his belt without checking how much money was in it. 'I shall share it with Nico,' he said. 'I couldn't have solved the mystery without him.'

'I will not accept any money,' I protested. 'I already earn a good wage and you need it for a very important cause, remember?'

'It was fun helping you solve the mystery,' said Mistress Fotini. 'If you're ever in Corinth again please come and visit. Who knows, we might get involved in another adventure.'

'Nico and I have been discussing our future,' said Thrax. 'We are determined to solve mysteries wherever we find them. But, as we discovered the other night when we were captured, we cannot do it alone. We need friends to help us, secret accomplices who will come to our rescue or supply us with much-needed information. We want you and Gaia to be the first members of our team.'

'How exciting,' said Mistress Fotini. 'A secret society of crime fighters that one day will stretch from one end of the Hellenic world to the other. All dedicated to the cause of bringing justice to those who have been wronged.'

'We're calling it the Medusa League,' I said.

Mistress Fotini's eyes flashed. 'The Medusa is my favourite mythical creature. She can be cruel if you oppose her but if you choose to respect her, she will protect you.'

'A Medusa painted above the front door is one of the only things Thrax remembers about his home.'

'Yes. My father hung it there for protection,' said Thrax. He held out the other two charms I had bought from the girl in the potters' district. 'This will be our official amulet.'

Mistress Fotini and Gaia slipped them over their necks. 'To the Medusa League. May justice win every time!'

Thrax and I said a final goodbye, then squeezed into the secret passage. The door closed gently behind us.

* * *

It was blisteringly hot on the road to Cenchreae and Master Ariston, seated on Ariana, kept asking for water. Ahead of us a long line of travellers moved at a snail's pace. We could hear the sailors singing again.

'Mothers wait
Although it's late
For their sons returning
One more stop
One more battle
One more journey
And we're home
And we're home!'

I walked in silence, my head full of thoughts and ideas. So much had happened in the last few days. Thrax had solved his first mystery and I had found a new purpose in life. I was going to be a writer, a proper one, not just a scribe who copied down other people's work.

My dear friend seemed deep in thought too. He was weighed down with Master Ariston's luggage and he also had a small birdcage under one arm. Ahmose had given him two of his homing doves as a present. They were to be the Medusa League's first messengers.

Late in the afternoon we came to the spot where we'd been attacked by bandits. The caravan stopped for lunch and Master Ariston lay on the grass for a nap. We were in no hurry. The *Danais* was not expected to dock till late in the evening.

Thrax pulled a small bundle out of his bag and thrust it into my hands. 'I bought you a little present.'

I opened the parcel with some excitement. Presents don't happen very often in my life. Thrax had bought me four sheets of thick papyrus, and a new reed pen.

'You can use them to write your first story,' said Thrax.

'Thank you,' I said, putting them carefully in my tool bag. 'I shall treasure them dearly.'

We washed the lunch dishes in the stream, remembering the horrific attack when Tanoutamon had died.

I spied something flashing in the water and picked it up. It was a ring, shaped like a snake biting on its own tail. Its eyes were two bright drops of lapis lazuli. 'Oh look. Someone must have dropped this in the stream.'

I offered it to Thrax on the palm of my hand. 'You take it. It will help buy your freedom.'

Thrax pushed my hand away gently. 'Thanks, but no. Whatever money I need, I will earn with my wits.'

'I won't keep it either,' I said. 'Whatever riches I earn, I shall do so by the power of my pen. But I know who can make good use of it...'

We hurried back to where we'd left our belongings and Thrax lifted one of the doves out of the cage. Gently, he tied the snake ring to its legs with a piece of string. Then he opened his hands and the dove soared up into the reddening sky, the ring on its foot flashing in the afternoon sunlight. It made the bird look like a phoenix rising out of the darkening earth.

'One day I will be free as that bird,' said Thrax.

'And just as dazzling,' I added. 'I pray to the gods that day will come quickly.'

We both watched the dove flying back to Ahmose until it was no bigger than the evening star. Master Ariston woke up and we continued towards Cenchreae and Captain Gorgos waiting for us on the *Danais*.

I thanked the gods for my good fortune as we sailed out of the harbour that night, the sky above us heavy with stars. Later, passing Salamina, I wondered what had happened to the angry sailor we had left in the harbour. He was to bring danger into our lives soon. But I didn't know that then. All I knew was that the gods had blessed me with so much in the last few days: a breathtaking adventure, a daring new friend and a new purpose in life.

I couldn't wait to get back to Athens, and to find a quiet corner in Master Lykos's house where I could set out my new sheets of papyrus and start writing my first story.

I already had a title for it: *The Mark of the Cyclops*.

Bonus Bits!

Greek gods

Thrax and Nico, the main characters in our story, lived in a period of Greek history known today as Classical Greece. It lasted from around 510 to 323BC. The age when myth and history merged was long gone. People still believed in the ancient gods, though. They prayed and sacrificed to them often and referred to them all the time. Here is a list of the gods mentioned in our story.

Aphrodite goddess of love and beauty. Her special symbol was the evening star. She was also associated with the sea and often depicted in art swimming with dolphins and swans or surrounded by pearls.

Apollo   god of music and poetry. A beautiful young man, his symbol was the lyre. When only four days old, Apollo was believed to have killed a serpent-like dragon called the Phyton.

Asclepius   god of healing. His symbol was a rod with two snakes wrapped around it. Some of his temples had sacred dogs that would lick the sick to heal them.

Athena   goddess of many things, including wisdom, mathematics, war and heroes. Her many symbols included the owl, the olive tree, the shield, the spear and a protective amulet with the Medusa's face on it.

Dionysus   god of wine, the grape harvest, merrymaking and theatre. Many illustrations of him show him as a well-rounded old man but he is sometimes drawn as a younger person too. He was looked after by magical rain nymphs when he was a child.

Hephaestus   god of blacksmiths, craftsmen and sculptors. He was also the protector of volcanoes and fire. Hephaestus was believed to have made the weapons for the gods in his special workshop on Mount Olympus. Despite being ugly, his wife was the ravishing Aphrodite.

Hera the mother goddess. She was married to Zeus, the chief god and was the protector of women, marriage and family. Believed to be a very serious person, she was often depicted on a throne. The peacock, the cow and the lily were some of her many symbols.

Hermes god of thieves, travellers and athletes. Believed to be quick on his feet and able to slip easily from the mortal world into the mystical one, he acted as a messenger for the other gods. He was also honoured as the god of boundaries between countries and worlds.

Iliythia goddess of childbirth and protector of midwives. She was usually shown in art holding a flaming torch. This was a symbol of the pain a mother endures during childbirth.

Poseidon god of the sea. He was also known as the earth-shaker because he could cause earthquakes. He could create islands and springs by striking rocks with his trident. Sailors prayed to him for protection while fishermen left their tridents in his temple when they retired.

Zeus   the chief god on Mount Olympus, he ruled over the other gods with a fiery temper. All the other gods rose to their feet when he was present. His special symbols were the oak, the bull and the thunderbolt, which he loved hurling at his enemies.

Glossary

Thrax and Nico use many Greek words in their first adventure. Here is a list of what they mean.

Acropolis fortified part of a Greek city, usually built on a hill

Agora market place, also used for public meetings

Andron special room where men relaxed and held parties

Archon magistrate or an important man in a city

Attica region in Greece

Aulos musical instrument made with two reed pipes

Chiton tunic, worn by both men and women

Chlamys   short woollen cloak

Diolkos   paved road along the Isthmus of Corinth

Gynaikeion   room in a house reserved for women

Hellas   Greek name for Greece

Himation   long woollen garment worn over the left shoulder

Kalamos   reed pen, usually with a split nib to hold the ink

Kottabos   party game where players flung wine at a basin

Symposium   party with music, entertainment and discussions

Trierarch   captain of a trireme

Trireme   war ship with three banks of oars

Pots and more pots!

Thrax and Nico come across many different kinds of Greek pottery in Corinth. Here are descriptions of some of them.

Alabastron   small perfume bottle, sometimes carried on a string

Amphora   large jar with two small handles. Used for storing wine, oil or food like olives and grain. One of the most common pots in ancient Greece.

Hydria   large water jug with a handle and a spout

Kantharos   big drinking cup with two large handles and a stemmed foot, used for drinking or for holding offerings

Krater   large bowl used for mixing water and wine at parties

Lekanis   small round dish with a lid for keeping little treasures and keepsakes

Lekythos   tall vase used for storing oil, often used as a grave marker

Loutrophoros   tall-necked vase used for bathing in weddings and funerals

Oinoche   huge round pouring jug, used for serving wine or water

Stamnos   squat vase used for mixing wine and water

Rhyton   ceremonial drinking cup, often shaped like an animal's head

Acknowledgments

There are a few people I must thank for helping to bring this story to the printed page: my agent Katy Loffman at Pollinger Ltd who believed in the project right from the start; Hannah Rolls at Bloomsbury for seeing the potential in Thrax and Nico and my editor Susila Baybars without whom the plot would be full of holes.

Thanks are also due to Albert Schembri who encouraged me to put aside my doubts and write something longer than I had ever attempted, and to my fellow members of the Scattered Authors Society who were there with advice, support and home-baked goodies when the going got tough.